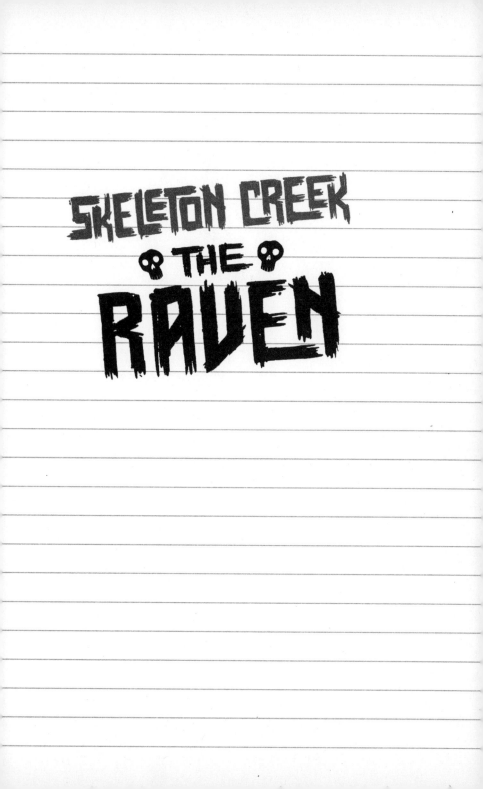

PATRICK CARMAN's
SKELETON CREEK
THE RAVEN

SCHOLASTIC PRESS
NEW YORK

PC STUDIO

Library of Congress Cataloging-in-Publication Data
Available
ISBN 978-0-545-24995-9

10 9 8 7 6 5 4 3 2 1   11 12 13 14 15

Printed in the U.S.A.   23
First edition, May 2011

The text type was set in GFY Thornesmith.
Book design by Christopher Stengel

Are you new to Skeleton Creek?

If so, my best friend, Sarah Fincher, has a secret place where a lot of our story is posted in the form of videos.

Scare easily? Leave the lights on.

SARAHFINCHER.COM
PASSWORD:
BRINGMEUPTOSPEED

IN AN HOUR THE WORLD WILL TURN DARK AND STILL. ANYONE WHO'S EVER CAMPED IN THE REMOTE WILDERNESS KNOWS WHAT I'M TALKING ABOUT. THERE ARE NO STREETLIGHTS IN THE WOODS. NO LAMPS, STOREFRONTS, OR GLOWING LAPTOP SCREENS. THESE THINGS ARE A COMFORT, EVEN IN A TOWN AS SMALL AS SKELETON CREEK, BUT I WON'T HAVE ANY OF THEM ONCE THE SUN GOES DOWN.

YOU MIGHT SAY, "YEAH, BUT THERE ARE STARS. ISN'T THAT THE SAME AS A BILLION FLASHLIGHTS? AND THERE'S THE MOON — THAT THING IS HUGE." TRUE, ON A CLEAR NIGHT WITH A FULL MOON IT'S NOT AS DARK IN THE WOODS, BUT THAT'S NOT THE KIND OF NIGHT I'M ABOUT TO SUFFER. I CAN ALREADY HEAR THE THUNDER CLAPS TEN MILES OR SO OFF IN THE DISTANCE. A STORM IS COMING AND CLOUDS ARE GATHERING OVERHEAD.

THERE WILL BE NO STARS OR MOON TONIGHT.

MY DAD AND I LEFT SKELETON CREEK EARLY THIS MORNING IN ORDER TO GET AWAY FROM ALL THE CRAZINESS IN TOWN. FOR THE PAST WEEK, THE PHONE HAD BEEN RINGING OFF THE HOOK FOR INTERVIEWS, AND

NEWS VANS HAD PULLED INTO TOWN FROM PORTLAND AND SEATTLE. FIRST, I'D FOUND GOLD ON THE DREDGE, THEN I'D DISCOVERED THE MISSING JEFFERSON LIBRARY RIGHT UNDER OUR NOSES. NO ONE KNEW HOW MUCH HELP I'D GOTTEN FROM SARAH, BECAUSE I COULDN'T TELL ANYONE. (SHE'S FAR TOO VALUABLE WORKING IN SECRET, AT LEAST UNTIL AFTER SHE MAKES THE LONG DRIVE HOME FROM LA TO BOSTON.) NOPE, THIS ONE WAS ALL ON ME. I WAS TURNING SKELETON CREEK INTO A TOWN KNOWN FOR ITS HIDDEN TREASURES, AND MY DAD THOUGHT IT BEST TO GET ME OUT OF DODGE BEFORE MY HEAD TURNED FREAKISHLY BIG.

"NOTHING LIKE ROUGHING IT TO PUT THINGS INTO PERSPECTIVE," HE'D SAID. "LET'S YOU AND ME HIGHTAIL IT FOR THE RIVER."

HE DIDN'T HAVE ANYTHING TO WORRY ABOUT, BECAUSE I DON'T HAVE ANY SPACE IN MY HEAD TO DWELL ON HOW AMAZING I AM. I'M PREOCCUPIED WITH MORE IMPORTANT THINGS, LIKE HOW I'M GOING TO STAY ALIVE FROM ONE DAY TO THE NEXT.

I'D DEVISED A COVER FOR HOW I'D COME TO FIND THE MISSING JEFFERSON LIBRARY BOOKS HIDDEN UNDER GLADYS MORGAN'S LIBRARY. INSTEAD OF A NOTE

HENRY LEFT IN THE DREDGE, IT WAS A SIMPLE MAP I'D FOUND WHILE HELPING DISGORGE FORTY MILLION IN GOLD FROM THE FLOORBOARDS. I HADN'T SHOWN THE MAP TO ANYONE BECAUSE . . . WELL, I JUST HADN'T. NO ONE SEEMS TO CARE ABOUT A LITTLE DECEPTION WHEN YOU'RE THE BEARER OF GOOD NEWS.

I FEEL PARANOID AND UNPROTECTED SO FAR AWAY FROM HOME. THE RAVEN, HENRY, THE GHOST OF OLD JOE BUSH — IT'S LIKE I'M BEING FOLLOWED BY AN ARMY OF ZOMBIES DEAD SET ON TRACKING ME DOWN.

IT ALL COMES DOWN TO THE SECRET CROSSBONES SOCIETY, AND THREE SHADOWY FIGURES AT ITS CORE.

FIRST, THERE'S THE A-POSTLE, THE CROSSBONES RECORDER. HIS CREEPY VIDEOS MADE IT CLEAR THAT CROSSING THE A-POSTLE CAME WITH A PRICE: HE'D REVEAL YOUR SECRETS TO THE REST OF THE WORLD. SARAH FOUND FOUR HIDDEN A-POSTLE MESSAGES ON HER DRIVE FROM BOSTON TO LA, WHICH WAS WHAT LED US TO DISCOVER THE MISSING BOOKS FROM THE JEFFERSON LIBRARY. THESE BOOKS WERE A CROSSBONES TREASURE, BUT THE A-POSTLE LED US RIGHT TO THEM FROM BEYOND THE GRAVE.

THEN, THERE'S THE GHOST OF OLD JOE BUSH, WHO ISN'T REALLY A GHOST AT ALL, BUT MY DAD'S FORMER FRIEND, HENRY. WHEREABOUTS UNKNOWN. I CAN'T SAY FOR SURE WHOSE SIDE HENRY IS ON, BUT TWO THINGS <u>ARE</u> CERTAIN: HE'S STILL OUT THERE AND HE'S SCARIER THAN EVER.

AND FINALLY, THERE'S THE RAVEN. THE MUSCLE. THE POWER. THE REALLY BAD DUDE. EVERY SECRET SOCIETY NEEDS ONE, AND THE CROSSBONES IS NO EXCEPTION.

I'VE THWARTED THE CROSSBONES ENOUGH TO KNOW: THE RAVEN WILL WANT ME DEAD. IT'S THE QUICKEST WAY TO STOP ME.

MY DAD DIDN'T EXACTLY DO ME ANY FAVORS BY DRAGGING ME DOWN THE RIVER ON A RAFT INTO THE MIDDLE OF NOWHERE. THE REALLY BAD THING ABOUT CAMPING IN THE DEEP OF THE WOODS? UNLESS YOU COUNT A SLEEPING BAG, THERE'S NO PLACE TO HIDE ONCE THE SUN GOES DOWN. MY FEARS CAN COME AT ME FROM WHATEVER DIRECTION THEY WANT.

HERE'S ANOTHER THING ABOUT CAMPING: THERE ARE AT LEAST FOUR WAYS TO DO IT, ONLY ONE OF WHICH QUALIFIES AS <u>REAL</u> CAMPING IF YOU ASK MY DAD.

How to camp, according to my dad, with actual fireside quotes included:

Option 1 (lamest): Use a Cabin

Dad: "The only way this counts as camping is if there's no indoor plumbing or beds, the nearest help is at least an hour drive down a dirt road, and the place is crawling with termites."

Option 2 (a near tie for lameness with option 1): Use an RV

Dad: "I think I just threw up."

Option 3 (barely not lame): Camp with a Tent in a Campground

Dad: "There's a guy delivering firewood for five bucks a box from the back of a golf cart. Why not bring a big-screen TV and a Lay-Z-Boy while you're at it?"

Option 4 (officially roughing it): Pack into a Remote Location, Fend for Your Life

Dad: "Give me three matches, my fishing gear, and some tinfoil. I'll live out here for a month and a half."

Which is how I found myself setting up my pack tent on the edge of the river five miles downstream from town, nowhere near a hamburger or a cell tower. I'd barely rolled out my sleeping bag before my dad was calling me to the edge of the water . . . as he always does.

"Ready for the flip?" he asked. I nodded, knowing before he flipped the coin up in the air that I had no chance. I'd lost seventeen out of seventeen coin flips on seventeen out of seventeen trips down the river, and things were not about to change.

"Heads," I called, just to give myself a fighting chance.

"Sorry, sport, it's tails. See there?"

The light wasn't very good and the show was awfully fast, but it did look like tails. Does he carry a two-tailed nickel around in his pocket and use some sleight of hand? I wouldn't put it past him. My dad loves fly-fishing enough to pull one over on his own kid, that much is for sure. Losing the flip meant he'd be catching our dinner while I rounded up firewood, and the light was fading fast.

For all his talk, my dad is often woefully unprepared in the wild. If it's fly-fishing you're looking for, he's your man. The boat is crammed full of fly boxes and other "essential trout gear." This is because he spends four hours getting the fishing gear ready, looks at his watch, and spends his last ten minutes packing everything else he'll need. When I leave to hunt for firewood I will be armed with only my wits and a hatchet, the blade of which is duller than a butter knife.

Looking up into the sky, I sense what's coming. By midnight it's going to start raining. In fact, from the smell of the air, I'd guess it's going to hail golf balls, the kind that will shred a pup tent and leave me trembling in my sleeping bag.

Better get with it so I don't end up traipsing around in the woods after dark and bump into a bear . . . or someone who's out to get me.

MONDAY, JULY 11, 11:30 P.M.

I'M BACK AT THE CAMPSITE IN MY ONE-MAN TENT. THE FIRE HAS ALL BUT GONE OUT — A FEW GLOWING EMBERS ARE ALL THAT REMAIN — AND ALL I CAN SAY IS THIS:

WHAT I DISCOVERED OUT THERE IS GOING TO MAKE THIS THE LONGEST NIGHT OF MY LIFE.

HE FOUND ME, OR I FOUND HIM.

NOISES OUTSIDE.

MONDAY, JULY 11, 11:35 P.M.

I think it's gone. Maybe it was just the wind. I don't know whether to look or stay inside. Praying.

I'M NOT CLOSING MY EYES UNTIL DAWN.

MY CELL PHONE ISN'T GOOD FOR A SIGNAL, BUT
IT DOES THROW OFF A SOFT BLUE LIGHT, WHICH IS
THE ONLY LIGHT I HAVE INSIDE MY TINY TENT. DAD
IS ALREADY SNORING IN HIS OWN COCOON FIVE
FEET AWAY.

OKAY, I'M GOING TO WRITE DOWN WHAT HAPPENED
SO I DON'T FORGET ANY OF THE DETAILS. NOTE TO
SELF: SET UP AN OVERNIGHT RECORDING CAMERA IN
MY ROOM WHEN I GET HOME IN CASE I GET AN
UNWELCOME VISITOR IN THE MIDDLE OF THE NIGHT. AND
BRING THE HATCHET TO BED WITH ME.

FOR SOMEONE WHO LIVES IN THE MOUNTAINS I
HAVE A SURPRISINGLY BAD SENSE OF DIRECTION. I GET
TURNED AROUND EASILY, WHICH IS EXACTLY WHAT
HAPPENED AS I MEANDERED OUT IN THE WOODS IN
SEARCH OF FIREWOOD. I'D FOUND A PRETTY HEFTY
ARMFUL OF FALLEN TWIGS AND BRANCHES AND SET IT
DOWN, GLANCING IN EVERY DIRECTION AS I TURNED IN
A CIRCLE.

WHERE WAS I? WHICH WAY HAD I COME FROM?

The woods grew menacingly quiet, and then I heard the sound of wood being split. Surely it was my dad, tired of waiting for my return as he set up a fire to cook the fish he'd caught. I picked up my collection of busted branches and twigs and started in the direction of the sound. It was farther off than I expected, but the sound kept getting louder, so I kept at it. I came to the edge of a clearing, where a single, gigantic tree stood alone in the gathering gloom. And then it struck me: My dad didn't have the hatchet. I had the hatchet.

It's not him I hear chopping.

There, at the base of the tree, was the cloaked figure of a man. Whoever it was wore an oversized, black rain slicker that ran from his knees all the way up over his head. The hood was pulled low over his face, a black tunnel that led to eyes I couldn't see. He had the biggest ax I've ever seen — it had to be five feet long with a blade as wide as my head. He swung as if in slow motion, broad and powerful, slamming against thick bark. I knew enough about

WOODCUTTING TO KNOW THAT EVEN WITH AN AX THAT BIG IT WOULD TAKE HOURS TO BRING DOWN SUCH A MONSTER, AND THE CLOAKED FIGURE HAD ONLY JUST BEGUN.

A THUNDER CLAP, LOUD AND CLOSE, BLASTED INTO THE VALLEY. I DROPPED THE WOOD I'D GATHERED, DASHING BEHIND A TREE FOR COVER. I THOUGHT ABOUT RUNNING, WHICH IS WHAT I SHOULD HAVE DONE. INSTEAD, I TOOK OUT MY PHONE AND HIT THE RECORD BUTTON, THEN PEERED AROUND THE EDGE OF THE TREE.

THE THUNDER CLAP HAD COVERED THE SOUND OF THE DROPPING WOOD. THE FIGURE CONTINUED SWINGING THE GREAT AX.

AND THEN, WITHOUT WARNING, HE STOPPED.

LIGHTNING FILLED THE SPACE BETWEEN US AND I SAW THAT HE WAS WATCHING ME. AND WORSE, HE WAS SHARPENING THE BLADE AGAINST A STONE, SPARKS FLYING AS THE SOUND OF THUNDER ARRIVED, AS IF ON CUE.

MY BACK AGAINST THE TREE, CHEST HEAVING, I THOUGHT ONCE MORE OF RUNNING. NIGHT WAS CLOSE AT HAND, AND THE LAST THING I WANTED WAS TO BE LOST IN THE DARK WITH AN AX-WIELDING MANIAC ON

MY TRAIL. I WAITED FIVE SECONDS, TEN, FIFTEEN. THE SOUND OF SHARPENING HAD STOPPED AND THE CHOPPING HADN'T STARTED UP AGAIN. MAYBE HE'D GIVEN UP ON THE BIG TREE. MAYBE HE HADN'T SEEN ME AFTER ALL. MAYBE HE'D GONE BACK INTO THE GLOOM.

WHEN I PEERED AROUND THE EDGE OF THE TREE ONCE MORE, HOPING TO FIND MYSELF ALONE IN THE WOODS, THE HOODED MAN HAD CREPT MUCH CLOSER. HE WAS CLOSE ENOUGH TO HIT ME WITH THE AX IF HE'D WANTED TO.

AND THEN HE SPOKE.

"STORM'S COMIN'."

HIS VOICE WAS RASPY AND COLD, HIDDEN UNDER THE CLOAK, AND I DIDN'T KNOW FOR SURE IF HE MEANT THE STORM OVERHEAD OR SOMETHING ELSE. HIS KNUCKLES WHITENED ON THE AX HANDLE — AN AX I NOW REALIZED WAS PAINTED BLACK.

"GONNA BE A BIG ONE," HE WENT ON. "DANGEROUS. NOT LIKE THE ONES BEFORE."

I JUST STOOD THERE, SPEECHLESS, STARING AT THE BLADE.

"BETTER TAKE COVER."

He lifted his head in the direction from which I'd come, as if to tell me where I'd find my dad and the camp we'd set up, and then he turned and walked away. I was struck then by how ghostlike he was as he passed by the huge tree and kept on until he disappeared into the shadows.

I looked at my hand, which still held my phone.

I'd recorded the whole encounter.

But even a recording won't answer the big question I have:

Was that the RAVEN?

MONDAY, JULY 11, 11:47 P.M.

I MADE IT BACK TO CAMP, GRABBING UP PIECES OF WOOD AS I RAN, AND SHOWED UP TO FIND MY DAD HAD ALREADY BUILT A FIRE FROM WOOD SCRAPS AND COOKED THE FISH.

"I WAS JUST ABOUT TO COME LOOKING FOR YOU," HE SAID, STARING AT THE PALTRY COLLECTION OF TWIGS I'D GATHERED UP. HE LOOKED INTO THE NIGHT SKY. "STORM'S COMIN'."

HE USED THE EXACT SAME WORDS AS THE MAN IN THE WOODS — STORM'S COMIN' — WHICH SENT A CHILL DOWN MY SPINE, ALL THE WAY INTO MY BOOTS. WE ATE QUICKLY, THREW TARPS OVER BOTH OUR TENTS, AND HUNKERED DOWN FOR WHAT WOULD BE A LONG, SLEEPLESS NIGHT.

STORMS IN THE MOUNTAINS OFTEN PASS THROUGH QUICKLY ON THEIR WAY TO SOMEWHERE ELSE, AS IF THEY'RE LATE FOR A POKER GAME AND THEY'VE ONLY STOPPED BY LONG ENOUGH TO PUT OUT YOUR FIRE. THIS WAS JUST SUCH A STORM — QUICK AND BRUTAL — HERE AND GONE IN TWENTY MINUTES FLAT. WIND WHIPPED THE TENTS, A MIX OF RAIN AND HAIL PUMMELED THE TARP, AND ALL THE WHILE I THOUGHT

ABOUT THE FIGURE I'D SEEN IN THE WOODS AND THE

MESSAGE HE'D DELIVERED.

THE RAVEN.

THE MORE I THINK ABOUT IT, THE SURER I AM.

THE FINAL PLAYER IN THE CROSSBONES GAME HAS

FOUND ME.

BUT WHAT DOES HE WANT FROM ME?

NEVER MAKE THE MEAN GUY MAD.

IT WILL COME BACK TO HAUNT YOU.

I NEED TO CALM MYSELF DOWN. I AM TRYING TO FIND SOME GOOD SIDE IN ALL THIS. AT LEAST IF THE RAVEN IS NEAR, HE CAN'T BE IN LA, SO SARAH IS SAFE FROM THE SWING OF A BLACK AX.

IT'S THE RAVEN'S JOB TO CLEAN UP MESSES, GET RID OF PROBLEMS, PROTECT CROSSBONES INTERESTS AT ALL COST.

ONE OF THE FIRST THINGS I THOUGHT OF WHEN I SAW THE RAVEN WAS FITZ, MY BUDDY WHO USED TO WORK AT THE FLY SHOP. THE RAVEN IS HIS DAD, SO OBVIOUSLY I'M WORRIED ABOUT HOW FITZ IS DOING. ARE THE TWO OF THEM LIVING UP HERE IN THE WOODS OR SOMETHING? DOES FITZ COME DOWN TO THIS VERY BANK ON THE RIVER AND CATCH FISH WHEN I'M NOT HERE?

I JUST PEERED OUTSIDE THE SLIT OF MY TENT, THINKING I MIGHT JUST SEE FITZ STANDING THERE, CASTING HIS LINE OVER THE WATER IN THE DARK. BUT THERE WASN'T ANYONE THERE.

I can hear the river but I can't see it. Funny how something I love so much during the day can turn so deadly. Like a black sludge drifting past, waiting to pull me under.

I could drown just like the Apostle and Old Joe Bush before him.

Water can be evil that way.

There's one more thing I need to say before I stop writing for the night and start staring at the ceiling of my tent, waiting for the ax to come down.

Fitz gave me an envelope before he and his dad left the trailer they lived in. Inside was a piece of paper he should not have given me — because it belonged to his dad.

Now that I think I've met the Raven, I understand what a risk it was to take that piece of paper.

Storm's comin'.

Gonna be a big one. Dangerous. Not like the ones before.

Better take cover.

I THINK THE RAVEN MIGHT KNOW I HAVE THIS PIECE
OF PAPER.

I THINK HE MIGHT FOLLOW ME RIGHT BACK INTO
TOWN AND USE THAT BLACK AX TO BUST DOWN MY
DOOR AND GET IT BACK.

LONGEST. NIGHT. EVER.

TUESDAY, JULY 12, 8:00 P.M.

MADE IT TO DAWN WITHOUT GETTING KILLED (VERY PLEASANT SUNRISE), FELL ASLEEP ON THE RAFT, WOKE UP AT THE TAKEOUT. BLEARY-EYED, I HELPED MY DAD LOAD THE BOAT AND THE GEAR ONTO THE TRAILER, WHICH MY MOM HAD SHUTTLED DOWN THE RIVER FOR US.

"YOU'RE LOOKING PRETTY HANGDOG, CHAMP," DAD COMMENTED WHEN WE PULLED INTO TOWN AND THE TRUCK CAME TO A STOP IN FRONT OF OUR HOUSE. "HOW ABOUT I PUT STUFF AWAY FOR ONCE AND YOU TELL MOM TO WRESTLE UP SOME DINNER? LOOKS LIKE THINGS HAVE CLEARED UP NICELY AROUND HERE."

I DIDN'T HESITATE, THIS BEING THE FIRST TIME IN MEMORY I'D BEEN LET GO WITHOUT HAVING TO CLEAN UP AFTER A TRIP. WHICH IS HOW I GOT TO WHERE I AM NOW: SITTING ON THE FRONT PORCH WHILE MY MOM COOKS UP A LATE DINNER FOR ME AND DAD.

APPARENTLY, MY DAD WAS RIGHT ABOUT GETTING OUT OF DODGE: THE REPORTERS HAVE MOVED ON,

LEAVING PHONE NUMBERS, IF WE HAPPEN TO THINK OF A SCOOP TO GIVE THEM. PROBABLY THEY GOT BORED OF OUR THREE RESTAURANTS AND ONE BAR, OR MAYOR BLAKE DROVE THEM HALF CRAZY WITH HIS AMBITIONS FOR THE TOWN. EITHER WAY, BESIDES A LIST OF REPORTERS TO CALL BACK, I'M A FREE MAN. SKELETON CREEK IS BACK TO NORMAL, AT LEAST FOR THE MOMENT.

"YOU SHOULD HAVE SEEN GLADYS MORGAN TAKE TO THE PRESS," MY MOM TOLD ME. "I'VE NEVER KNOWN THAT WOMAN TO TALK FOR SO MANY MINUTES IN A ROW IN ALL MY LIFE."

WE CHATTED ABOUT THE BOOKS AND THE TOWN LIBRARIAN, THE FISHING AND THE STORM THAT BLEW THROUGH, BUT I COULDN'T BRING MYSELF TO MENTION THE MAN IN THE RAIN GEAR. I COULDN'T TELL HER OR MY DAD. I DON'T EVEN KNOW WHY. I MEAN REALLY — WHY <u>NOT</u> TELL THEM? I GUESS IT FEELS LIKE ONCE I DO IT'LL LEAD TO SARAH, AND WHEN THAT HAPPENS EVERYTHING WILL COME CRASHING DOWN AROUND US.

I DON'T FEEL LIKE A LIAR. MORE LIKE A

WITHHOLDER OF CERTAIN FACTS. I HAVE TO BELIEVE THERE'S A DIFFERENCE. THEN AGAIN, IT'S JUST LIKE A LIAR TO MAKE A DEADLINE FOR WHEN HE'LL START TELLING THE TRUTH.

WE JUST NEED A LITTLE MORE TIME TO BRING THIS CROSSBONES THING TO A CLOSE. A WEEK, MAYBE TWO, AND I'LL TELL THEM EVERYTHING. IT'S JUST THAT FIRST I HAVE TO GET SARAH BACK HOME WITH A FEW UNSCHEDULED STOPS ALONG THE WAY — STOPS I HAVEN'T EVEN FIGURED OUT YET.

AS SOON AS I CAN SCARF DOWN SOME DINNER, I'VE GOT SOME WORK TO DO. FOR STARTERS, I'M PUTTING THE WEBCAM ON MY LAPTOP INTO FULL SWING STARTING TONIGHT. EVEN IN LOW-RES RECORDING MODE IT'LL FILL HALF MY HARD DRIVE OVERNIGHT, BUT AT LEAST I'LL KNOW IF SOMEONE IS WATCHING ME. WITH ALL THESE NEW PEOPLE FLOATING IN AND OUT OF TOWN AND THE RAVEN HIDING IN THE WOODS, WHO KNOWS WHO MIGHT TRY TO SET UP THEIR OWN SURVEILLANCE ON ME?

I need to reach out to Sarah as fast as I can. Her film camp runs four more days, then she's driving back home to Boston. I need to email her the Raven sighting I recorded, get her take on the man in the rain slicker. But I also need to send her a scan of the <u>other</u> Raven. Being up all night in a tent at least gave me a chance to really look at it carefully. It's no less confusing than the Skull Puzzle, which led us to the missing Jefferson library books. Maybe this Raven Puzzle will lead to an even bigger mystery.

It's two sided, same as last time. But somehow, it's even scarier looking than the Skull Puzzle.

Flames, haunted roads, castle towers, a nickel? Where does a guy begin solving a puzzle like this? There is one image that's a dead giveaway: the nickel. That's Thomas Jefferson's old home, Monticello. It's in Virginia. At least we know one of the locations the Apostle is trying to lead us to, even if

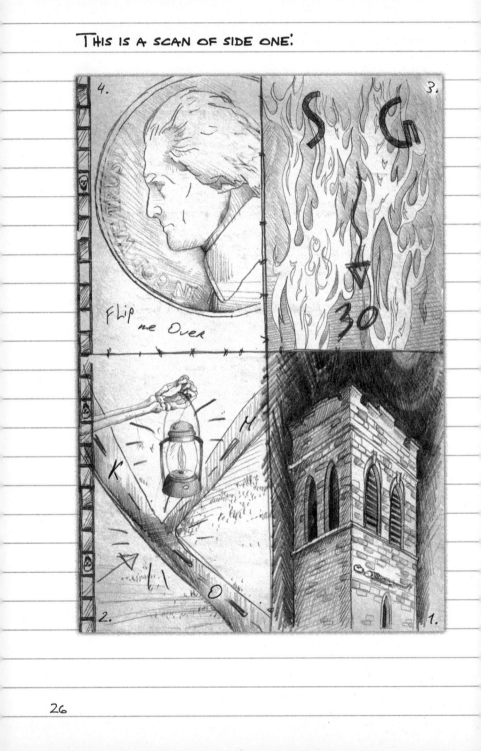

SARAH WILL HAVE NO IDEA WHERE TO LOOK ONCE SHE GETS THERE.

THE SKULL FROM THE EARLIER PUZZLE HAS BEEN REPLACED BY A RAVEN, THE FOUR CORNERS BY CLUES I CAN'T EVEN BEGIN TO UNDERSTAND. GHOST ROOM FLOORS, STONE MARKERS, WISPS OF WIND — THE A-POSTLE'S METHODS OF RECORDING DEFINITELY LEAN INTO THE BIZARRE. BUT THERE IS ONE ENCOURAGING BIT OF NEWS ON THIS SIDE OF THE RAVEN PUZZLE: THE WORDS.

WEST TO EAST AND FOLLOW THE TRAIL OF THE A-POSTLE! TELL ME THAT LONG AGO, THE A-POSTLE WAS ON A JOURNEY VERY MUCH LIKE THE ONE SARAH IS ON NOW. ORIGINALLY, HE WENT EAST TO WEST, WHICH WE ALREADY KNEW. BUT NOW WE'RE FINDING OUT HE ALSO TRAVELED WEST TO EAST, DROPPING CLUES ON HIS WAY BACK. WHICH MEANS SARAH CAN DO THE SAME THING.

IF WE CAN FIGURE OUT WHAT THE CLUES MEAN, SARAH CAN FOLLOW THE TRAIL OF THE A-POSTLE ALL THE WAY BACK TO BOSTON.

AND WE MIGHT JUST FIND THE MOST VALUABLE CROSSBONES TREASURE OF THEM ALL.

28

My worries?

The Apostle is trying to trick us.

The ghost of Old Joe Bush will haunt our every move.

And the Raven will try to stop us.

TUESDAY, JULY 12, 10:00 P.M.

I FINALLY GOT TO MY ROOM AFTER A DINNER OF COLD CHICKEN, POTATO SALAD, AND RED JELL-O WITH TINY MARSHMALLOWS FLOATING INSIDE. I FIRED UP THE LAPTOP AND FOUND TWO EMAILS FROM SARAH. QUICKLY, I READ THEM, DELETED THEM, AND SCRUBBED THE MEMORY FOR TRACES OF CONTACT. MY PARENTS HAVE BACKED OFF A LITTLE ON THEIR FEELINGS ABOUT ME COMMUNICATING WITH SARAH, BUT JUST THE SAME, I CAN'T TAKE ANY CHANCES THEY MIGHT BE CHECKING IN ON ME.

Ryan,

I wish I could have been there when they smashed up the library. I'd have paid top dollar to watch Gladys Morgan freak out. Word is out about the books you found. Jefferson library — nice — we're kind of amazing, I guess. Wish I could be there to take some of the credit. My parents are like, "Did you hear about Ryan McCray?" I wanted to say, "Um, yeah, I know all about it. I found most of the clues!" But we both know I couldn't do that.

I took your voice mail seriously, Ryan. What did Fitz give you? What makes you think it will lead to something else? Don't leave me hanging!

Film school is getting better. I'm holding my own. My last video beat the socks off the one from this eleven-year-old prodigy who's been schooling me. Three more days and it's good-bye Hollywood, back in the car for the long haul to Boston.

Call me the second you get off that stupid river! It's getting lonely out here without you.

Sarah

THIS IS THE PROBLEM WITH LONG-DISTANCE COMMUNICATION: MOST OF IT HAPPENS DIGITALLY. VOICE MAILS, EMAILS, TEXT MESSAGES — THOSE ARE THE CURRENCY OF MY SECRET ONGOING CONNECTION TO SARAH FINCHER. ADD TO THAT THE ISOLATION OF THE RIVER OUTSIDE SKELETON CREEK AND THE INSANE SHOOTING SCHEDULE SARAH IS KEEPING AND IT'S A MIRACLE WE TALK AT ALL. THE BEST I COULD DO BEFORE LEAVING WITH MY DAD HAD BEEN A QUICK MESSAGE:

Don't tell anyone you were involved. Fitz left me something we need to talk about. Heading for the river — not by choice! — will email the moment I get back.

SARAH'S SECOND EMAIL WAS MORE BLUNT.

ˈWHERE ARE YOU? And don't tell me you're still fishing. Not buying it. S.

I SENT SARAH THE RAVEN VIDEO, ALONG WITH THIS NOTE:

Sarah,

Sorry I disappeared. My dad made me do it!

Are you ready for another haunted road trip? I've attached scans of what Fitz left for me. Looks like we have our work cut out for us.

And it gets worse.

The Raven found me.

I attached a video that speaks for itself.

Miss you TONS. Be careful out there. Hope filming is going well.

R.

Tuesday, July 12, 11:11 p.m.

11:11, a bad omen. I hate when I look at the clock and find numbers doubled up like that. Gives me the creeps.

Sarah must have been sitting at her computer editing video clips when I emailed because she responded less than twenty minutes later.

She posted the video of the Raven in the woods. Seeing what I recorded, along with the additions Sarah made from past sightings, just about knocked me off my chair. At the end, she starts analyzing the Raven Puzzle.

It appears she's already hot on the Apostle's trail.

If something's happened to me, and someone is reading this after I've disappeared (or worse), get to a computer and take a look.

You can meet the Raven for yourself.

It will help you realize what we're up against.

SARAHFINCHER.COM
Password:
MELANIEDANIELS

WEDNESDAY, JULY 13, 11:00 A.M.

No rest for the weary.

My dad was pounding on my door at 7:00 and yelling for me to get out of bed, breakfast was on the table. Sometimes I hate that he opened a fly shop in town financed by a fraction of the gold I found on the dredge. Maybe if I'd left that gold there I'd still be sleeping right now and my dad would be out of town at his old job. Times like these, it feels like the world is caving in on me, like I need a secret corner where I can be alone with my thoughts.

After I watched Sarah's video last night I tried to stay awake, but I was just too exhausted from the night before. The good thing about being that tired? I slept like the dead, just what I needed. I was refreshed, ready to figure this thing out while my dad is away from the shop all day on a float.

When I left the house this morning, my mom gave me a list of reporters to call.

"Get it done, kiddo. If you don't, they'll just keep calling the house," she told me, shaking her

36

HEAD. "THE MAYOR IS THE WORST OF THE BUNCH. HE CALLED FOUR TIMES YESTERDAY LOOKING FOR YOU."

WHY AM I NOT SURPRISED? FIRST THE DREDGE, NOW THE JEFFERSON LIBRARY BOOKS. MAYOR BLAKE IS A SHAMELESS PROMOTER WHEN IT COMES TO GETTING SKELETON CREEK ON THE MAP. A LOT OF FOLKS ARE STARTING TO WONDER IF HE'S GUNNING FOR A BIGGER POSITION, LIKE MAYOR OF BOISE OR GOVERNOR OF THE ENTIRE STATE. I CAN ALREADY IMAGINE THE PLATFORM HE'D RUN ON:

CITY INCOME IN SKELETON CREEK UP 10,000 PERCENT. JOB GROWTH THROUGH THE ROOF. TOURISM EXPLODING.

HE WON'T MENTION THAT ANY OF THIS HAD TO DO WITH MY FINDING THOMAS JEFFERSON'S MISSING BOOKS, AND MILLIONS IN GOLD. SOMEHOW, LIKE EVERY POLITICIAN, HE'LL MAKE IT SOUND AS IF HE HAD AN AWFUL LOT TO DO WITH IT.

MY DAD TOOK OFF WITH A RETIRED COUPLE FOR A FEW HOURS, MUMBLING TO HIMSELF ABOUT WHAT A DAY IT WAS GOING TO BE WITH TWO PEOPLE BORED ENOUGH TO TRY FLY-FISHING FOR THE FIRST TIME. HE GUESSED THEY'D BE EXPERTS AT TANGLING UP THEIR LINES AND

CASTING INTO THE TREES. IT'S ALWAYS A TOUGH DAY ON THE RIVER WITH A HUSBAND AND WIFE WHO DON'T KNOW WHAT THEY'RE DOING. I ACTUALLY FELT SORRY FOR HIM AS HE LEFT, LEAVING ME TO WATCH THE SHOP ALL DAY. HE WAS NICE ENOUGH NOT TO MAKE ME TIE FLIES WHILE HE'S GONE, WHICH IS SAYING SOMETHING SINCE HE'LL PROBABLY GO THROUGH A DOZEN AN HOUR WITH THOSE TWO. LOOKING AT THE LIST OF REPORTERS I WAS SUPPOSED TO CALL DIDN'T EVEN MAKE ME WANT TO TRADE WITH HIM — IT WAS THAT BAD ON A RAFT WITH AN OLD COUPLE, ZERO FISHING EXPERIENCE BETWEEN THEM.

THE FIRST INTERVIEW WAS WITH THE PHILADELPHIA ENQUIRER, A NICE LADY WHO WAS MORE EXCITED THAN I WAS ABOUT THE DISCOVERY OF THE BOOKS. SHE HAD A COOL ACCENT AND SHE LAUGHED A LOT. APPARENTLY, SHE'D BEEN AN AMATEUR SLEUTH FOR YEARS HERSELF AND ENVIED MY FINDING SUCH AN IMPORTANT TREASURE. TWO MORE EAST COAST PAPERS, THE ASSOCIATED PRESS, THE OREGONIAN, THE SEATTLE TIMES, THE BOISE HERALD — ALL OF THEM ASKING THE SAME QUESTION OVER AND OVER AGAIN: HOW'D YOU KNOW WHERE TO LOOK?

I DODGED THIS LINE OF QUESTIONING BETTER WITH EVERY PHONE CALL I MADE, BUT IT WAS HARD NOT TO LIE. MOSTLY, I PLAYED DUMB JUST TO BE SAFE, WHICH MADE ME A SUPER LAME INTERVIEWEE (THIS TENDS TO SHORTEN UP THE CONVERSATIONS).

I'VE STILL GOT THREE MORE PAPERS TO CALL, SMALLER ONES, I THINK, BUT I'M STARVING. PLUS, I WANT TO GO LOOK AT THE GAPING HOLE IN THE LIBRARY FLOOR AGAIN.

WEDNESDAY, JULY 13, 1:21 P.M.

THE HOLE IS STILL THERE.

It's STILL BORING, TOO.

WHY ANYONE WOULD THINK RIPPED-UP FLOORBOARDS IN AN OLD LIBRARY WOULD MAKE A GOOD TOURIST ATTRACTION IS BEYOND ME, BUT IF SOMEONE CAN SELL IT, THAT SOMEONE IS MAYOR BLAKE. AND HE'S GOT ENOUGH MONEY IN THE SKELETON CREEK COFFERS TO PUT A NICE ROPE AROUND IT AND GO ALL INTERACTIVE, SO THAT WILL HELP.

WAIT — SPEAKING OF MAYOR BLAKE, HE JUST WALKED INTO THE FLY SHOP.

AND HE'S NOT ALONE.

48

"This here's Mr. Albert Vern," the mayor said when he came in. His southern accent has kicked up a notch, a sure sign he really is thinking about running for higher office. "You'll never guess where he's from. Go on now, guess!"

I guessed he was from the Boston Red Sox, recruiting me to play baseball.

Albert Vern looked at me as if to say, "Quite a mayor you've got here. You wouldn't happen to know how I could get away from him, would you?"

"The Washington Post!" the mayor told me, completely proud of himself for hobnobbing with national media. "Mr. Vern is from the Washington Post! Ain't that something else? Right here in Skeleton Creek. And it gets better — he's staying for the whole week!"

I nodded and tried to act friendly, but my insides were churning. In fact, they're still churning. I don't need a big-city reporter hanging around, watching my every move. If he's working for the Post, he must be pretty good at snooping out the truth.

41

"Do you have any golden stone flies with rubber legs?"

This was the first thing Albert Vern asked me, which led the mayor to glance at him like he'd lost his way coming through town and needed directions. It didn't take long for me to realize Albert Vern was an outdoorsman when he wasn't reporting.

"I can hardly wait to get out on the river" were his next words, the mayor's cue to leave us fishermen alone.

"You two get to know each other. That's real good. I'll be just outside, checking my messages."

Mr. Vern sighed with relief when Mayor Blake was gone, explaining that he'd already endured a tour of the town and an exhaustive description of recent events.

"Tell me what's working and I'll take a dozen," he said, explaining that he'd long been a traveling reporter for the <u>Post</u>, casting a line on rivers from New York to western Canada. "I could tell you a fishing story or two."

42

I WAS REALLY STARTING TO LIKE THIS GUY. NO TOUGH QUESTIONS, JUST A REQUEST FOR THE BEST FLIES WE HAD TO OFFER.

"SOMETHING WRONG WITH YOUR BACK, MR. VERN?" I ASKED, STARTING TO WARM UP TO A FELLOW WRITER. HE WAS TWISTING AROUND LIKE THERE WAS A KINK IN HIS SPINE.

"THREW MY BACK OUT PICKING UP MY BAG AT THE AIRPORT — HAPPENS ALL THE TIME. I'M USED TO IT."

"HOW LONG DOES IT LAST?" I ASKED. THE POOR GUY LOOKED FEEBLE, LIKE I COULD KNOCK HIM DOWN WITH MY PINKIE FINGER.

"USUALLY A DAY OR TWO. BUT I THINK THE MOUNTAIN AIR IS HELPING. I'LL BE FINE."

A REAL TROUPER, THIS GUY, WHICH I ALSO LIKED, BUT THEN THE QUESTIONS STARTED.

"SO YOU'RE THE ONE WHO FOUND THE MOST FAMOUS MISSING BOOKS IN THE WORLD?"

I BEGAN PICKING OUT FLIES, DROPPING THEM INTO A PLASTIC CONTAINER.

"IT WAS AN ACCIDENT, REALLY. I JUST HAD A FEELING, MR. VERN."

43

He laughed and I could tell it jolted his back by the look on his face that followed.

"Well, I hope you have the same feeling about those flies you're picking out. I'd like to land some fish tonight."

He asked me to call him Albert and hoped we could go fishing together one evening, just talk about this and that. He was more interested in a vacation than a story, or so he said. Casting, he told me.

I have to be very careful with this guy. I can imagine slipping up and saying something I shouldn't or being just stupid enough to show him the Raven Puzzle if I need help. The river has a way of lulling my senses to sleep.

Before I could worry too much, Mayor Blake rang the bell on the door, returning from checking the messages on his phone. Albert Vern paid for his flies, and the two of them left for pie. The shop would be quiet for at least an hour — the perfect time to do some research.

For once, I wanted to beat Sarah to the punch.

Wednesday, July 13, 4:12 p.m.

BINGO on the first location! And more good news to boot.

First, the drawings I figured out.

The Ghost Room:

And the tower with the skeleton inside.

An hour of searching online for skeletons in churches and castles led me nowhere. Turns out there are thousands of castles, even more churches, and . . . let's see . . . billions of

SKELETONS. NOTHING WORTH REPORTING ON GHOST ROOMS, EITHER. I WAS AT A DEAD END, AND I ACTUALLY THOUGHT ABOUT DOING SOME WORK AROUND THE SHOP. LUCKILY, EDGAR ALLAN POE CAME TO THE RESCUE. THE OLD DUDE SAVED ME ONCE AGAIN.

I HAD BEEN LOOKING MOSTLY AT THE TOWER AND THE SKELETON, BECAUSE THAT WAS MARKED NUMBER 1. MY HOPE WAS THAT NUMBER 1 MEANT CLOSEST TO THE WEST COAST: THE FIRST STOP ON SARAH'S JOURNEY BACK HOME.

THE IDEA OF A SKELETON LYING IN A STONE BUILDING STARTED TO GET ME THINKING ABOUT "THE CASK OF AMONTILLADO," A WICKED COOL POE STORY I'VE READ AT LEAST A DOZEN TIMES. IT'S A STORY WHERE ONE GUY LURES ANOTHER GUY DOWN INTO THIS CHAMBER, THEN CHAINS HIM UP DOWN THERE (YIKES!). AFTER THAT, THIS NUT JOB BUILDS A STONE WALL IN FRONT OF THE OPENING, SO THERE'S, LIKE, THIS SMALL ROOM WITH A MAN CHAINED UP INSIDE. THE GUY STARTS FREAKING OUT, BUT THE STONES ARE PRETTY THICK SO NO ONE CAN HEAR HIM SCREAMING. I GUESS HE GOES CRAZY AND STARVES TO DEATH BEHIND THE WALL OR TONS OF RATS FIND HIM. AT LEAST THAT'S WHAT I THINK HAPPENS.

EITHER WAY, IT TOTALLY CLUED ME IN! THE
SKELETON IN THE TOWER WASN'T JUST LYING THERE.
IT WAS _IN_ THE WALL, JUST LIKE IN THE STORY. SO I
STARTED SEARCHING FOR MASONS WHO WENT MISSING,
GHOST STORIES REVOLVING AROUND MISSING PEOPLE,
LEGENDS OF PEOPLE BEING BURIED ALIVE IN TOWERS AND
CHURCHES.

THE CRAZY THING ABOUT WHAT I DISCOVERED?
THE STORY OF THIS TOWER HAS SOME EERIE
SIMILARITIES TO THE MADE-UP STORY OF
"AMONTILLADO." AND THERE'S A LOT OF INFORMATION
OUT THERE ABOUT IT, TOO.

THE TOWER IS PART OF ST. MARK'S CHURCH IN
CHEYENNE, WYOMING.

BUILDING ON THE CHURCH STARTED IN 1868, AND
THE MAIN STRUCTURE WAS FINISHED WITHOUT ANY
DISTURBANCES. EIGHTEEN YEARS LATER, PEOPLE STARTED
CLAMORING FOR A BELL TOWER. THEY WANTED A
REAL SHOWSTOPPER, SOMETHING NO ONE IN THE AREA
COULD BUILD, SO THEY IMPORTED TWO MASONS FROM
SWEDEN WHO KNEW WHAT THE HECK THEY WERE DOING.
JUST LIKE IN POE'S STORY — TWO GUYS!

IT GETS BETTER.

48

So these two masons worked on the tower for a while until one day the church parson, Dr. Rafter, came by to check on the work. When he did, there was only one mason, not two, and the one guy was acting strange.

The next day? Both masons were gone. (Cue thunderbolt.)

It was more than thirty years before they started building again, which is when the real trouble started. The new masons heard unexplained hammering in the walls and words they couldn't understand drifting into the air. Churchgoers swore they heard a whispered message they could understand:

<u>There is a body in the wall!</u>

Jump ahead to 1966, when a very old man showed up at the church to confess his sins. He confessed (I'm not making this up!) that when he was a young mason, he and a fellow Swede were hired to build the tower, but his friend fell down the stone stairs leading to the basement and broke his neck. Afraid he'd be tried for murder, the remaining mason stuffed the body

AGAINST ONE OF THE UNFINISHED WALLS. THEN HE USED CEMENT AND STONES AND BASICALLY BUILT THIS DEAD GUY INTO THE TOWER ITSELF.

I GOTTA SAY . . . THAT'S JUST WRONG. AND SO EDGAR ALLAN POE IT'S NOT EVEN FUNNY.

THE REVERSE SIDE OF THE RAVEN PUZZLE HAS THIS DRAWING:

A.

Ghost
Room

THE GHOST ROOM. THAT'S A REAL PLACE IN
ST. MARK'S CHURCH. UPSTAIRS IN THE TOWER, A
ROOM WHERE VOICES COME THROUGH THE WALLS. AND
UNDER ONE OF THE FLOORBOARDS?

A MESSAGE FROM THE APOSTLE.

DAD'S HERE. DANG. GOTTA GO.

WEDNESDAY, JULY 13, 10:07 P.M.

When my dad got back from the river he put me to work unloading the boat. The retired couple had broken a shop record, losing thirty-one flies on their way down the river. To top it off, they lost a fly rod — not on a big fish, which we would have cheered. No, the husband just dropped it right in the river and let it float away. How is this even possible, you ask? It requires a rare set of circumstances, but it does happen.

First, you need a beginner who's sure he can outfish his beginner wife.

Second, that guy needs to be sitting in the back of the raft, where the oarsman can't see him without turning around. (That'd be my dad.)

And last, you need a clumsy person known for dropping expensive things off of buildings and into rivers and then trying to hide it from everyone for approximately thirty seconds.

That's about how long it takes for a two-hundred-dollar fly rod to vanish from view in a moving river.

On the upside, they paid for the rod and were good tippers, which made my dad feel a little better.

"I should have known what was happening. It was real quiet for about twenty seconds. Never a good sign," my dad said. "Why don't they just tell me when they drop a fly rod? I could swim out and get it."

"If it was you and mom on the boat, would you tell?" I asked.

My dad rubbed the stubble on his chin and smiled. "Good point."

He milled around the shop, checking messages and sales on the till.

"I hear you had a visitor from the Washington Post."

I asked him how he knew about Albert Vern and he said the mayor had left three messages on his phone while he floated out of cell range.

"Sounds like this guy's a fisherman."

After that my dad informed me that the mayor had offered to pay full price for an all-day float down the river.

"But only if you guide him," my dad added.

I could hardly say no. Number one, a day on the river with someone who knows how to fish and loves doing it is hard to come by when you're a guide. A large percentage of gigs are with people who have no business being on a river to begin with. And the guy seemed pretty cool, so why not?

"I could use a day in the shop after today," my dad said, sounding a little worse for the wear. "You go, I'll tie up three dozen flies and set up a new guide rig. It'll be a win-win."

At that moment, all I really wanted to do was stay in the shop and do research all day. The faster we figured out all the locations Sarah would need to visit, the sooner we'd know if it was even possible.

The trail led to something, somewhere. Could be an even bigger stash of gold for all we knew.

I got through dinner and "porch time" with my mom while the lazy summer evening took my dad into dreamland. When I got to my room I set the webcam on my laptop to record

54

THROUGHOUT THE NIGHT, AND CALLED SARAH. SHE PICKED UP ON THE FIRST RING AND I EXPLAINED EVERYTHING ABOUT THE HAUNTED CHURCH LOCATION BEFORE SHE COULD GET A WORD IN EDGEWISE.

"CHEYENNE, WYOMING," SHE SAID. "NOT EXACTLY ON THE WAY HOME, BUT NOT TOO FAR OFF THE PATH, EITHER."

I EXPLAINED THAT I'D RUN THE NUMBERS — IT WAS ELEVEN HUNDRED MILES FROM LA TO CHEYENNE. ABOUT SIXTEEN HOURS BY CAR.

"HOW COME YOU GET ALL THE CUSHY GIGS AND I HAVE TO DRIVE LIKE A MANIAC ALL OVER KINGDOM COME?" SHE ASKED.

"AT LEAST YOU DON'T HAVE TO DEAL WITH REPORTERS AND RETIRED FISHERMEN," I SAID. THEN I DESCRIBED ALBERT VERN AND TOMORROW'S FISHING EXPEDITION.

"DON'T TRUST REPORTERS," SHE WARNED. "HE SOUNDS LIKE A SMOOTH OPERATOR. SPILL THE BEANS AND WE'LL NEVER GET TO THE END OF THE APOSTLE'S TRAIL."

I AGREED COMPLETELY, BUT WHAT I WAS REALLY WORRIED ABOUT WERE THE OTHER LOCATIONS AND HOW

SHE WAS GOING TO CONVINCE HER PARENTS TO GO OFF ROUTE ON THE WAY BACK TO BOSTON.

MY MOM KNOCKED SOFTLY ON THE DOOR AND I HUNG UP BEFORE SHE ENTERED WITHOUT BEING INVITED IN. SHE'S LIKE THAT, MY MOM. THE VERY SOFT KNOCK ISN'T SO MUCH A COURTESY AS AN EXCUSE TO SAY, "I WARNED YOU I WAS COMING IN — DIDN'T YOU HEAR ME KNOCKING?"

SHE ASKED TO SEE MY PHONE, WHICH SURPRISED ME, SINCE I'D GOTTEN THE FEELING THEY WERE SLACKING ON KEEPING AN EYE ON ME. I SHOULD HAVE KNOWN BETTER. THERE WAS NO HIDING WHO I'D CALLED.

"MUST BE HARD, HAVING HER AS CLOSE AS LOS ANGELES."

"IT'S OKAY," I LIED.

"JUST DON'T DO DOING ANYTHING STUPID, OKAY? YOU KNOW HOW YOUR FATHER WILL REACT IF THINGS GET OUT OF HAND AGAIN."

"GOT IT. NO PROBLEM."

SHE HANDED BACK MY PHONE, BUT NOT BEFORE SAYING I SHOULD RECONSIDER RECONNECTING WITH MY OLD FRIEND. "REMEMBER HOW MUCH TROUBLE YOU both got into before?" she asked. As if I was about to forget.

Still, I could tell she understood. Your best friend is your best friend, and besides, how much trouble could we get into when we lived so far apart?

Actually, quite a bit.

Thinking about it now, I realize this is where it gets kind of scary. Like, maybe we really ARE stepping over a line we shouldn't. Part of me says, Hey, Sarah is seventeen, what's the big deal? She drove all the way out to LA by herself. She's an independent kind of girl. Her mom and dad aren't strict like mine. But another part says we shouldn't be pulling one over on our parents the way we are.

I called her back, and Sarah's answer, regarding the detour on the way home, was: "I already talked to them and they're fine with it."

Sarah had already called and asked about sidetracking to different locations. The haunted road trip documentary had been a big hit at the camp and her instructor was hoping for part two

ON THE WAY BACK. SARAH HADN'T PICKED ALL HER LOCATIONS YET, BUT SHE DEFINITELY WANTED TO VISIT ST. MARK'S CHURCH.

"IT'S IN THE RIGHT GENERAL DIRECTION," SARAH EXPLAINED. "AND HOW MUCH TROUBLE CAN I GET INTO IN WYOMING, ANYWAY?"

I GOT THE FEELING SHE WAS PRETTY GOOD AT CONVINCING HER PARENTS TO LET HER STRAY A LITTLE BIT. AS FAR AS THEY COULD TELL, SHE WAS BEING RESPONSIBLE. WHAT I WOULDN'T GIVE FOR PARENTS LIKE THAT. I'M LUCKY MY DAD WILL LET ME RUN THE RIVER, LET ALONE GET IN A CAR AND DRIVE ACROSS THE COUNTRY LOOKING FOR HAUNTED HOUSES.

TURNS OUT SARAH WAS ALSO MAKING SOME PROGRESS OF HER OWN ON THE RAVEN PUZZLE.

"I'M NOT A HUNDRED PERCENT SURE, BUT I THINK I KNOW WHAT'S GOING ON WITH THE SECOND LOCATION. LET ME WORK ON IT SOME MORE AND I'LL EMAIL YOU."

IN CLASSIC SARAH FASHION, SHE WOULDN'T BUDGE ON ANY DETAILS. SHE ONLY TOLD ME THAT IF SHE WAS RIGHT, THEN THEY WERE INDEED HEADING BACK EAST ON THE APOSTLE'S TRAIL.

The last thing she said had me a little worried.

"He's here," she told me.

"Who is?"

"Him. The ghost of Old Joe Bush, Henry, whoever."

"How do you know?"

"I just do. I can feel it. I think he's following me."

"Oh."

Oh? Was that the best I could do?

What do you say when your best friend tells you she thinks a man possessed by a ghost is following her across the country?

THURSDAY, JULY 14, 2:20 A.M.

I JUST WOKE UP AND I FEEL LIKE SOMEONE HAS BEEN
WATCHING ME.

   NOT A GOOD FEELING.

THURSDAY, JULY 14, 6:30 A.M.

BAD! BAD! BAD!

THREE HOURS OF LYING IN BED AND FINALLY THE SUN STARTED COMING UP AT 5:00 A.M. SO I COULD SET FOOT ON MY FLOOR WITHOUT BEING TERRIFIED SOMETHING WOULD PULL ME UNDER THE BED. SARAH AND I BOTH HAVE THAT SIXTH SENSE, WHERE WE CAN FEEL IT WHEN WE'RE BEING WATCHED, AND CRAWLING OUT OF BED A HALF HOUR AGO, I WAS SURE SOMEONE HAD BEEN IN MY ROOM. THERE'S A BIG PART OF ME THAT WISHES I HADN'T SET MY WEBCAM TO RECORD THROUGH THE NIGHT. THEN I COULD JUST <u>IMAGINE</u> WHAT WAS IN MY ROOM. THERE WOULD BE A PART OF ME THAT COULD THINK IT WAS A CAT OR THE WIND BLOWING, THAT NOTHING SINISTER HAD TAKEN PLACE.

BUT I DID RECORD WITH MY WEBCAM. I EVEN USED THAT FUNKY NIGHT-VISION SETTING THAT TURNS EVERYTHING GREEN AND SHADOWY.

MY SPOOK METER TOLD ME THAT SOMETHING HAD HAPPENED AROUND 2:00 A.M., SO I STOPPED THE SIX HOURS OF FOOTAGE I HAD AT AROUND 1:50 A.M. AND SLOWLY WORKED THROUGH THE NEXT TEN MINUTES.

NOTHING AT 2:00 A.M.

61

Nothing between 2:00 a.m. and 2:05 a.m. At 2:06 a.m., all the blood drained out of my face.

The door creaked open, and then, for, like, ten seconds, nothing.

Then it moved into the room and leaned over the desk.

The Raven had entered my house.

The picture went black for a moment, then he was back, towering over my bed, staring at me in that huge, hooded rain slicker.

The camera went dark again, longer this time. When the picture came back, the Raven had moved to my bookshelf. A few seconds later he was gone.

There's something awful about being watched in my sleep. It's like I'm helpless. I can't defend myself against a giant ax if I'm asleep!

I'll tell you one thing: No more sleeping without a baseball bat or the hatchet from the camping supplies.

I just hope I don't accidentally swing at my dad or my mom if they check on me after midnight.

62

I SENT SARAH THE WEBCAM FOOTAGE. MAYBE SHE CAN DO SOME ENHANCEMENTS AND SEE SOMETHING I DIDN'T. HE WAS LOOKING FOR THE RAVEN PUZZLE AT MY DESK AND ON MY BOOKSHELF, I'M SURE OF IT.

DID HE TAKE ANYTHING?

DID HE KNOW I WAS RECORDING HIM?

AND MOST IMPORTANT, IS HE PLANNING TO OFF ME IN MY SLEEP?

WHEN I LOADED MY EMAIL TO SEND THE WEBCAM VIDEO, THERE WAS A LONG MESSAGE WAITING FOR ME FROM SARAH.

Ryan,

I know what the second clue means. Totally figured it out. The really good news? It's in the southeast corner of Kansas, heading in the right direction. And it's only a few hours from Little Rock. Remember when I came out here? Little Rock is where my mom's old college roommate lives. I can stay there again. It's all working out.

So here's the deal with the second location, which has the greatest name in the history of haunted locations: the Spooksville Triangle. Nice! Here's that section of the Raven Puzzle:

2.

See how each of the three roads have a letter on them? That was the giveaway. K is for Kansas, M for Missouri, and O for Oklahoma. That means the location is right where the three states meet. After I figured that out, it was easy finding the Spooksville Triangle. It's everywhere online! A very well known haunt.

The skeleton hand with the lantern represents the ghost, but you'll have to look it up on your own. I gotta go make a movie!

More soon,

Sarah

We're getting good at this. Two days with the puzzle, and three locations down:

— Monticello, Jefferson's old haunt in Virginia
— St. Mark's Church in Cheyenne, Wyoming
— The Spooksville Triangle, corner of Kansas, Missouri, and Oklahoma.

I have no idea what we're supposed to do at any of these places or what we'll find, but it's a good start.

I spent fifteen minutes online, and Sarah was right; there's a ton of stuff about the Spooksville Triangle out there. Legend has it that a girl wandered away from her parent's farmhouse and got lost, so the mom went out at night with a lantern searching for her. But the little girl never turned up. Now people go out there and see the Spooksville light, this unexplainable ball of orange that floats around in the field. Thousands of people have seen it, but no one has been able to explain what it is. The

GHOST OF THE MOM, OUT THERE WITH THE LANTERN, STILL LOOKING FOR HER DAUGHTER? IT WOULD SEEM SO.

THE SKELETON HAND HOLDING THE LANTERN OBVIOUSLY REPRESENTS THE MOM, THE THREE ROADS

REPRESENT EXACTLY WHAT SARAH SAID. THE OTHER
SIDE OF THE PUZZLE MAKES SENSE, TOO:

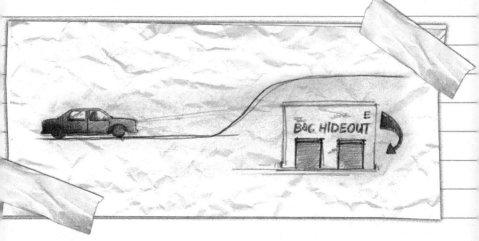

THE CAR AT THE BOTTOM OF THE ROAD — THAT'S
JUST LIKE THE LEGEND SAYS. IF YOU PARK ON THIS
DESERTED ROAD WHERE IT RISES IN FRONT OF YOU,
THAT'S WHERE YOU'LL SEE THE LIGHT AT NIGHT.

THE STONE MARKED E AT THE HIDEOUT FOR
B AND C.

THERE MUST BE AN OLD BUILDING OR SOMETHING
OUT THERE THAT CAN BE SEEN FROM WHERE YOU'D
PARK YOUR CAR. AND AT THE BACK RIGHT CORNER OF
THE BUILDING? A STONE MARKED A. NOW THAT'S
WHAT I CALL PROGRESS.

Meanwhile, I need to be at the shop early and set up for my day on the river. I'm looking forward to getting out of Dodge for the day, but I'm also nervous. We'll be floating right past the campsite me and my dad stayed at two nights ago.

And beyond the campsite, the clearing and the giant tree.

And the Raven with his five-foot black ax.

I hope I don't find him standing in the river up to his knees, waiting for my boat to drift by.

He's been in my house, so I wouldn't put it past him.

THURSDAY, JULY 14, 4:45 P.M.

LONG DAY WITH A FEW THINGS TO REPORT. JUST GOT DONE UNLOADING THE BOAT AND I'M AT THE CAFÉ ON MAIN. ORDERED A BURGER, FRIES, A COKE. I DON'T FEEL LIKE GOING HOME YET.

FIRST OFF, I GOT A CALL FROM SARAH AND SHE LEFT A MESSAGE, WHICH I TOLD HER NOT TO DO UNLESS SHE HAD TO. IT WAS NICE THOUGH. I'VE LISTENED TO IT THREE TIMES.

"HOW ARE YOU DOING? YOU MUST BE FREAKING OUT. I JUST — I CAN'T BELIEVE HE WAS IN YOUR ROOM. IF I WAS THERE YOU COULD STAY AT MY HOUSE OR SOMETHING. I FEEL TERRIBLE FOR YOU. PLUS, I MISS YOU. IT'S LONELY OUT HERE SOMETIMES.

"DO YOU THINK YOU SHOULD TELL YOUR PARENTS? I MEAN, THIS IS GETTING CRAZY, RIGHT? IT MIGHT NOT BE WORTH IT.

"I POSTED THAT VIDEO. YOU CAN FIND IT USING THE DICKENS PASSWORD. I THINK YOU MIGHT HAVE MISSED SOMETHING, UNLESS YOU JUST DIDN'T TELL ME.

"THE RAVEN LEFT SOMETHING BEHIND.

"OKAY, CALL ME, RIGHT? LET ME KNOW YOU'RE OKAY.

69

"Hug.

"Sarah."

It's nice to be missed. What I wouldn't give to sit up all night working out clues together. But that's not about to happen. I feel bad she's lonely. And I've been thinking the same thing all day: I need to tell my parents. The Raven stepped over the line by coming into the house. That was WAY out of bounds. I guess this entire thing will be taken up by the authorities (whoever they are) and the game of cat and mouse will come to a screeching halt. Sad, really. Sarah and I are so close to the end.

What's she mean about the Raven leaving something for me? Now I feel like I should have skipped the hamburger and gone home for dinner. At least I'd be one step closer to my laptop and whatever was left behind in my room. Then again, I'd have to endure dinner with my mom and dad, and right now, I'm afraid I'll come uncorked and tell them everything.

Quick recap of the fishing trip: It was awesome. I could stop there, but for future

REFERENCE, ALBERT VERN CAN FISH WITH ME
ANYTIME. HE ARRIVED AT THE SHOP WITH THE
MAYOR TWO STEPS BEHIND, HOUNDING ME TO CALL
THE <u>SEATTLE TIMES</u> TO ANSWER SOME OF THEIR
FOLLOW-UP QUESTIONS. IT WAS THE LAST THING I
WANTED TO DO, AND ALBERT WAS COOL ENOUGH
TO TELL THE MAYOR WE WERE LATE GETTING ON
THE RIVER ALREADY (NOT ACTUALLY TRUE) AND THE
INTERVIEWS WOULD HAVE TO WAIT. THE MAYOR,
PERPETUALLY BOWLED OVER BY A REPORTER FROM
THE <u>WASHINGTON POST</u>, SLINKED AWAY, BUT NOT
BEFORE PLEADING WITH ME TO MAKE THE CALL AS SOON
AS I GOT OFF THE RIVER. (CHECK THAT, DID IT AT THE
SHOP. MORE BORING ANSWERS THAT GOT ME OFF
THE LINE THREE TIMES FAST).

MR. VERN'S BACK HAD STRAIGHTENED UP AND HE
WAS RARING TO GO. HE WORE A SMILE ALL DAY,
FISHED LIKE A TRUE ENTHUSIAST, AND TIPPED LIKE A
GRANDPARENT. (IN OTHER WORDS, HIS TIP PAID FOR
MY DINNER AND THEN SOME.) HE ONLY ASKED A FEW
QUESTIONS, WHICH I DEFLECTED WITH EASE. IT MIGHT BE
HE'S JUST TRYING TO GET ON MY GOOD SIDE BEFORE
GRILLING ME WITH THE REAL ZINGERS. MAYBE THAT'S

WHAT REALLY GOOD REPORTERS DO — SOFTEN YOU UP BEFORE BREAKING OUT THE HEAVY ARTILLERY.

"You know, I have a mind to do this again tomorrow," he said when we pulled back in and my dad was there waiting for us.

"That can be arranged," my dad answered, and I could see in his eye that one day off the river was one day too many. If Albert Vern did go out again, it would be with my dad and I'd be left in the shop.

Fine by me.

I just ate an entire hamburger and a plate of fries in under five minutes and burped so loud the waitress called me a cow. Ouch.

Better get back home, see what Sarah found.

THURSDAY, JULY 14, 5:40 P.M.

MAYOR BLAKE IS GETTING DOWNRIGHT ANNOYING.
WHEN I GOT HOME HE WAS SITTING ON THE PORCH
EATING MY MOM'S LEFTOVER JELL-O WITH
MARSHMALLOWS IN IT. HE SAID HE WAS THERE JUST TO
VISIT, BUT I KNEW BETTER. WITHIN TEN SECONDS HE WAS
ASKING IF I'D CALLED THE SEATTLE TIMES. IF I DIDN'T
KNOW BETTER, I'D SAY HE'S GOT SOMETHING UP HIS
SLEEVE. MAYBE HE'S EVEN CAUGHT UP IN THIS WHOLE
CROSSBONES THING. NEVER TRUST A POLITICIAN.

IT TOOK FOREVER TO GET RID OF HIM AND CALL IT
AN EARLY NIGHT ON ACCOUNT OF COMPLETING MY
BEST FISHING DAY OF THE YEAR. MY DAD GRUNTED AT
ME, SAID TOMORROW WOULD BE EVEN BETTER, AND I
HIGHTAILED IT FOR MY ROOM.

SARAH AND I HAVE A FEW SECRET PASSWORDS
WE'VE SAVED UP IN CASE SHE NEEDS TO LEAVE ONE LIKE
SHE DID ON THE PHONE. THE "DICKENS PASSWORD" IS
ONE WE'VE HAD SAVED UP FOR A WHILE: EDWINDROOD.

I'M NOT GOING TO GET INTO WHAT WAS ON THE
VIDEO UNTIL WHOEVER IS READING THIS JOURNAL
CHECKS OUT THAT VIDEO. MAYBE I'M DEAD AND GONE,
DONE IN BY THE RAVEN, AND MY EXCLUSIVE STORY

HAS BEEN GIVEN TO ALBERT VERN AT THE WASHINGTON POST. WOULDN'T THAT BE SOMETHING? MR. VERN, IF YOU'RE READING THIS, YOU'RE A HECK OF A FISHERMAN. I'LL SEE YOU ON THAT BIG RIVER IN THE SKY WHERE THE FISH ARE ALWAYS BITING.

YOU MIGHT BE SENSING THAT MY MOOD HAS BRIGHTENED. I CAN'T TELL WHY UNTIL YOU WATCH WHAT SARAH POSTED. CRAZIEST VIDEO EVER.

DO THAT, THEN COME BACK. I'LL BE WAITING.

SARAHFINCHER.COM
Password:
EDWINDROOD

THURSDAY, JULY 14, 6:10 P.M.

WATCHING THAT VIDEO THE WAY SARAH EDITED IT DOWN JUST ABOUT SENT ME RUNNING THROUGH THE HOUSE SCREAMING FOR MY MOM. I WISH I WAS KIDDING. THE SECOND TIME THROUGH, WHERE SHE MESSED WITH THE LIGHTING, IT WAS OBVIOUS THE RAVEN HAD PUT A NEW BOOK ON MY SHELF.

IT DIDN'T TAKE ME LONG TO FIND IT, BECAUSE MOST OF MY BOOKS ARE PAPERBACKS.

THIS ONE IS OLD, AND IT'S GOT A HARDBACK SPINE, ONE OF THOSE CLOTH COVERS.

I SET IT ON MY DESK AND STARED AT IT FOR ABOUT A MINUTE.

THERE'S NO WRITING ANYWHERE ON THE OUTSIDE, AND THERE AREN'T VERY MANY PAGES.

MY FIRST THOUGHT? THIS THING IS LOADED WITH TOXIC YELLOW GAS THAT WILL POUR OUT THE SECOND I OPEN THE COVER, LIKE IN ONE OF THOSE ANCIENT BATMAN SHOWS. BUT CURIOSITY GOT THE BETTER OF ME AND I CAREFULLY LIFTED THE COVER.

NOTHING.

I DON'T MEAN NOTHING HAPPENED. I MEAN THERE

WAS NOTHING INSIDE. I FLIPPED THROUGH THE YELLOWED PAGES WITH MY THUMB AND THEY WERE ALL BLANK. IT WAS LIKE A GHOST BOOK — NOTHING ON THE SPINE, NO WORDS OR DRAWINGS OR PICTURES INSIDE. THE WHOLE THING WAS FORTY-TWO PAGES.

NEW YORK GOLD AND SILVER GAVE EACH OF ITS ASSETS A NUMBER BEFORE THE COMPANY WENT BELLY-UP A LONG TIME AGO. ONE OF ITS ASSETS WAS THE SKELETON CREEK DREDGE. AND ITS NUMBER?

42.

COINCIDENCE? SOMEHOW I DOUBT IT. WITH THE CROSSBONES, EVERYTHING IS CONNECTED. EVERYTHING HAS A MEANING.

THERE'S SOMETHING ELSE. AT THE VERY BACK OF THE BOOK, AFTER THE FORTY-SECOND PAGE, I FOUND TWO SHEETS OF FOLDED PAPER.

A DEATH THREAT FROM THE RAVEN?

I SAT THERE AND TOLD MYSELF NO MATTER WHAT KIND OF MESSAGE I WAS ABOUT TO READ I WAS ABSOLUTELY GOING STRAIGHT DOWNSTAIRS AND TELLING MY PARENTS EVERYTHING. I THOUGHT ABOUT THE CROSSBONES THREE-PART MISSION:

1) PRESERVE FREEDOM.
2) MAINTAIN SECRECY.
3) DESTROY ALL ENEMIES.

<u>DESTROY ALL ENEMIES</u> WAS SOUNDING VERY POSSIBLE, WITH ME AS THE ENEMY. I HALF EXPECTED THE RAVEN TO JUMP OUT OF THE PAGES OF THE BOOK AND THE GHOST OF OLD JOE BUSH TO CRASH THROUGH THE WINDOW.

THEY'D GET ME FROM BOTH SIDES.

I OPENED THE LETTER — SINGLE SPACED ON TWO SHEETS — AND KNEW IMMEDIATELY WHO IT WAS FROM. I'D SEEN THIS HANDWRITING BEFORE.

Hey, Ryan,

I saw you at the clearing the other day. I was hiding up on the ridge, keeping an eye on my dad. He's been going into Raven mode lately, which is never a good thing.

We're living up in this cave by the peak. Dang cold at night. He says we won't be here much longer, but I don't know. It feels like something's about to happen. Something big.

There's this metal box he's been carrying around forever. He keeps it pretty close, usually under his mattress. And the key is always around his neck. Yesterday we were out chopping wood together and he sent me back to the cave to refill a jug of water. I was there alone and I knew where he'd hidden it. I mean, I didn't actually see him hide it, but I heard him piling rocks in the corner of the cave on our first night up here. He thought I was sleeping, but I wasn't.

I moved all the rocks and found the metal box, hit the lock with my ax. It took three big swings, but the lock finally busted off. I don't know why I did it. He's going to find out. He'll know it was me. I guess I was tired of the secrets. I thought maybe there was something in there that would get me out of this cave and back on the football team, know what I mean?

There were two things in the box, neither of which makes any sense. One was a completely blank piece of paper. Well, there were two words at the top, but that was it.

The words?

THE CLAUSE.

A clause with no words. What the heck does that mean?

There was also a book inside with nothing but blank pages. So the mysterious metal box had basically nothing inside.

Makes me wonder if my dad is losing his marbles.

Or maybe there's something to this stuff I can't understand on my own.

I'm giving you the book, hoping you can help me. I have no idea why it's got no words or why it's so special, but trust me: It's a Crossbones treasure. Yeah, I know about the Crossbones. Been dealing with it my whole life. I bet it's why my mom bolted before I was three. She couldn't take all the secrecy. And you know what? I'm getting pretty sick of it myself.

Let's figure this out, Ryan. Let's pull one over on these guys.

I have a feeling we don't have much time. My dad's going to check the metal box at some point, and when he finds his stuff missing, I'm not sure what will happen.

I'm going to head into town and leave the book in your room while my dad's sleeping. I can't do much from way up here in the woods, but I'll do what I can.

There's a big divot in that giant tree my dad was chopping in the grove. If you find out anything useful, leave me a note there. I'll check the tree every day.

Or maybe just drop me a note sometime. It's pretty lonely up here.

Bring this whole crazy thing to an end, will you? And watch your back. I don't know what my dad is capable of anymore.

Fish on!

Your friend, Fitz

So it wasn't the Raven, after all. It was Fitz in my room last night! He sneaked into my room in the middle of the night in his dad's rain slicker and nearly scared me half to death. Wow.

I feel sorry for the guy. Must be rough living in a cave with the Raven. It makes me wonder what I'd do if I were him. Also makes me happy I have parents who aren't cave-dwelling secret-society members. What's a guy like Fitz supposed to do? I wish he could come down out of that cave and go back to work at the fly shop.

I can't help seeing the similarities between the tree and the blue rock, where Sarah and I used to exchange private notes. Is it just me, or do I have a habit of making friends who like to keep secrets from their parents? Getting to the blue rock was easy when Sarah wanted to exchange a note, but exchanges with Fitz will be harder. I can mountain bike down the river trail, but it's over an hour to the campsite on a bike, even longer coming back upstream.

Communicating with Fitz is going to be some work.

81

I called Sarah and spoke in my quietest whisper as I flipped the delicate pages in the book back and forth. She couldn't believe the book was totally empty, but she was thrilled about the fact that the Raven hadn't actually broken into my house. There was a pause on both ends and I knew what she was thinking. Know why? Because I was thinking the exact same thing.

If the Raven didn't come into my house, then he hadn't crossed some imaginary line Sarah and I had both set up in our heads. We could wait a little longer before telling anyone what we were doing. We could follow the trail of the Apostle and see where it led.

All we had to do was figure out one more clue — number 3 on the Raven Puzzle — and we'd know the road Sarah would need to follow.

Somehow I had a feeling it would lead back to the empty book I held in my hand. And the clause, whatever THAT was.

Friday, July 15, 6:55 p.m.

My parents are out playing cards down the street with the Muntzes (old family friends), so I've got a couple of hours to languish in my journal. Things to write have been piling up, but the time and energy to write them down have been few and far between.

Someone blabbed about the great fishing — probably the retired couple, even though they barely caught a thing — and the shop has been humming with fishermen ever since. Albert Vern seemed to sense the crush descending on Skeleton Creek and decided to call off the second-day float and head into Portland on a different assignment. He's supposed to be back early next week, after things die down, when Mayor Blake says I better get my act together.

"Time to get this story off the griddle before it leaves town for good" was how he phrased it.

I have some major news to report, but first I just gotta write down this Gladys Morgan

MOMENT — IT'S A CLASSIC. SHE CAME INTO THE SHOP YESTERDAY DURING A BRIEF LULL. I HALF EXPECTED TO SEE HER PULL AN AX OUT FROM BEHIND HER BACK AND START TAKING SWINGS AT OUR FLOOR TO EVEN THINGS UP AFTER WHAT WE'D DONE TO HER LIBRARY. BUT THE ANCIENT TOWN LIBRARIAN HAD OTHER THINGS ON HER MIND.

"DON'T THINK FOR A MOMENT YOU CAN FOOL ME. I KNOW EXACTLY WHAT YOU'RE UP TO," SHE WARNED ME. I WAS LIKE, <u>UH—OH. WHAT DOES SHE KNOW?</u>

"IS THERE SOMETHING I CAN HELP YOU WITH, MS. MORGAN?" I ASKED, GLANCING OVER AT MY DAD, WHO WAS STARTING TO PAY CLOSER ATTENTION THAN I WAS COMFORTABLE WITH.

"I'LL GET YOU BACK, RYAN MCCRAY, JUST YOU WAIT," SHE WENT ON. SO IT WAS ABOUT RIPPING HER FLOOR APART? OR NOT?

"UM, MS. MORGAN, I HAVE NO IDEA WHAT YOU'RE TALKING ABOUT."

SHE GLARED AT ME OVER HER BIFOCALS.

"HOW DUMB DO YOU THINK I AM?" SHE POINTED AT ME FIRST, THEN MY DAD. "START CARRYING YOUR

84

weight with these reporters! Do you have any idea how many calls I'm taking? How many interviews I've done? The mayor is at my heels all day while you fish or talk about fishing or sell fishing stuff to a bunch of fishing idiots. Get with the program!"

She turned on her heels and stormed out of the shop before my dad or I had a chance to answer her. Then we both started laughing.

"I'm standing right here!" she yelled from the front steps of the shop, the sound of our laughter drifting out the front windows and into the parking lot.

Other than that, the moments of levity have been rare. I spend most of my time worried about Fitz, the ghost book, the Raven Puzzle, sneak attacks by the Raven, being haunted by Old Joe Bush, and mostly about Sarah. She's acting reckless again and it's making me nervous.

She called me a little over an hour ago from an Arctic Circle somewhere in Nevada.

"An Arctic Circle in the desert," I said. "You've officially lost your mind."

"Arctic Circle the _restaurant_, not the north pole or whatever. A little trivia for you: They invented fry sauce. Pretty cool, huh?"

She was slurping on a drink they serve called a Lime Rickey.

"I thought you were in LA until tomorrow morning?" I asked.

She told me the camp had ended at noon, and that she was scheduled to stay the night in the dorm, then start the drive home tomorrow. Instead, she left the second the last class got out so her parents wouldn't get suspicious.

"Wait a second. I thought you said your parents were on board," I prodded her. I got a long pause followed by a shifty answer.

"They _are_ on board. They just want me off the road by nightfall, so that's kind of a problem."

"Tell the truth, Sarah. What's going on?"

She hemmed and hawed, then spilled it.

"Okay, so maybe I didn't tell them _everything_. They're fine with the detours on the way home, but they won't let me drive at night. That's

CRAZY, RIGHT? LIKE DRIVING IN THE DARK IS A BIG DEAL OR SOMETHING."

RIGHT ABOUT THEN I WAS SIDING WITH SARAH'S PARENTS. I COULD IMAGINE HER BREAKING DOWN AT MIDNIGHT ON THE SIDE OF THE ROAD IN THE MIDDLE OF NOWHERE, THUMBING A RIDE INTO SOME BACKWATER TOWN. NOT A GOOD THOUGHT.

"THEY BOOKED ME A HOTEL IN CHEYENNE FOR TOMORROW NIGHT," SARAH EXPLAINED. "BUT IT'S A SIXTEEN-HOUR DRIVE IF ALL I DO IS STOP TO USE THE BATHROOM AND GRAB A SANDWICH. I WOULD'VE HAD TO HAVE LEFT AT FIVE IN THE MORNING TOMORROW TO GET THERE BEFORE DARK, BUT THAT WOULDN'T HAVE GOTTEN US WHAT WE NEED, WHICH IS WHY THERE'S A DAY MY PARENTS DON'T KNOW ABOUT."

I DID THE CALCULATIONS IN MY HEAD: SARAH TOOK OFF FROM LA IN THE EARLY AFTERNOON, SO SHE WAS GOING TO ARRIVE AT ST. MARK'S CHURCH BETWEEN THREE AND FOUR IN THE MORNING TONIGHT.

"IT'S PERFECT, RYAN. THINK ABOUT IT: I'LL GET TO OUR FIRST LOCATION BEFORE THE SUN COMES UP, INSTEAD OF WHEN THE SUN IS GOING DOWN. I'LL FIND THE CLUE, THEN CHECK INTO THE HOTEL EARLY AND SNOOZE

ALL DAY. TECHNICALLY, I'M STILL CHECKING IN BEFORE DARK. RIGHT?"

ANYTIME SOMEONE STARTS A SENTENCE WITH THE WORD TECHNICALLY, IT'S A COVER FOR A LIE THAT'S ABOUT TO FOLLOW.

"I DON'T KNOW, SARAH — IT ALL SOUNDS KIND OF DANGEROUS. WHAT IF YOUR INSTRUCTOR CALLS THEM AND SAYS YOU LEFT EARLY?"

SHE TOLD ME IT WAS LA, WHERE FREE SPIRITS ROAM, AND THAT HER INSTRUCTOR WAS A HIPPIE WHO HAD ALREADY FLED TO THE BEACH FOR THE WEEKEND. THEN SHE CALLED ME A CHICKEN.

"NAME-CALLING IS BENEATH YOU," I SAID.

"SORRY, IT'S JUST . . . COME ON, RYAN. THIS IS IDEAL. I CAN PRACTICALLY SEE THE NEXT A-POSTLE VIDEO NOW. DON'T YOU WANT TO KNOW WHAT HE'S GOING TO SAY?"

SHE WAS ON HER GAME, FOR SURE. I WAS CURIOUS. AND I WAS HOLDING US BACK, AS USUAL.

SO I DID A LITTLE CALCULATING OF MY OWN, SEEING WHERE THIS WAS GOING.

"LET ME GUESS: YOU'LL WAKE UP IN WYOMING AROUND FOUR IN THE AFTERNOON AND CALL TO CHECK

IN WITH YOUR PARENTS, BECAUSE THAT'S WHEN YOU'RE SUPPOSED TO BE CHECKING IN."

"NOW YOU'RE GETTING IT. I'LL HIT THE ROAD RIGHT AFTER I CALL THEM, WHICH SHOULD PUT ME AT THE SPOOKSVILLE TRIANGLE IN MISSOURI BY TWO IN THE MORNING. AND I'LL GET PLENTY OF SLEEP. THIS WAY I CAN BE AT THESE LOCATIONS AT NIGHT, WHEN NO ONE IS AROUND. MAKES SENSE, RIGHT?"

IT WAS HARD TO ARGUE WITH SARAH'S LOGIC, BUT I WAS WORRIED FOR HER AND TOLD HER SO, ESPECIALLY SINCE SHE'D BEEN FEELING AS IF THE GHOST OF OLD JOE BUSH WAS SOMEWHERE NEARBY.

HER ANSWER TO THAT WASN'T AS SURPRISING AS I'D EXPECTED IT TO BE.

"I DON'T KNOW. TO TELL YOU THE TRUTH, I THINK HE'S ON OUR SIDE."

IT'S POSSIBLE. WHETHER IT'S MY DAD'S OLD FRIEND HENRY OR A GHOST OR SOME TWISTED VERSION OF THE TWO, IT'S POSSIBLE HE ISN'T TRYING TO HARM US ANYMORE.

BUT HOW CAN WE BE SURE?

"JUST GET TO CHEYENNE AS SAFELY AS YOU CAN," I SAID. "AND NO MORE SURPRISES."

I TOLD HER I'D BE AWAKE ALL NIGHT LONG, THAT SHE COULD CALL ME ANYTIME, AND THAT SHE BETTER CALL ME ONCE SHE GOT TO ST. MARK'S CHURCH. IF SHE BROKE DOWN SOMEWHERE SHE SHOULD CALL ME FIRST AND WE'D FIGURE IT OUT TOGETHER. AND IF SHE GOT TIRED, I ADVISED HER TO STICK HER HEAD OUT THE WINDOW AND SCREAM.

IT'S GOING TO BE A LONG NIGHT.

I'VE GOT TIME TO KILL.

I GUESS I'LL GO GRAB A FEW MOUNTAIN DEWS AND GET BACK TO THE RAVEN PUZZLE. IF SARAH IS GOING TO DO ALL THE EXPLORING, THE LEAST I CAN DO IS FIGURE THIS THING OUT FOR US.

THE MAYOR FOLLOWED MY PARENTS DOWN MAIN STREET AFTER THE CARD GAME AND GAVE ME YET ANOTHER LIST OF NEWS OUTLETS TO CONTACT WITH FOLLOW-UP QUESTIONS. HE SAID HE'D GIVE THEM TO GLADYS MORGAN IF I WANTED, SO I SNATCHED THE PIECE OF PAPER OUT OF HIS HAND. I DIDN'T NEED THE TOWN LIBRARIAN RETURNING TO THE FLY SHOP WITH A SLEDGEHAMMER.

WHEN THE MAYOR LEFT, I SAT ON THE PORCH WITH MY PARENTS FOR A HALF HOUR OR SO. I YAWNED ABOUT EVERY FIVE SECONDS AND FINALLY MY MOM TURNED TO MY DAD AND SAID, "YOU'RE WORKING THAT BOY TOO HARD."

MY DAD THOUGHT THAT WAS ABOUT THE DUMBEST THING HE'D EVER HEARD. HE WENT INTO ONE IF HIS YARNS ABOUT HOW HARD LIFE HAD BEEN IN THE OLD DAYS. IT WAS ALL I COULD DO TO NOT THROW UP.

MY DAD YAWNED AFTER THAT, THEN I DID, THEN HE YAWNED AGAIN.

"I'VE HAD BETTER CONVERSATIONS WITH TWO STRAY DOGS," MY MOM SAID.

A FEW MINUTES LATER, MY DAD HAD FALLEN ASLEEP ON THE PORCH, AND MY MOM HAD HER NOSE IN A BOOK, WHICH WAS MY CUE TO CALL IT A NIGHT.

WHEN I GOT TO MY ROOM, I FOUND THREE TEXT MESSAGES WAITING FOR ME, ALL FROM SARAH.

8:17 P.M.

<u>REST STOP, MAKING GOOD TIME, SUN WILL BE DOWN SOON. I'M WIDE AWAKE!</u>

9:45 P.M.

<u>WHITE CASTLE! NEED I SAY MORE?</u>

9:52 P.M.

<u>ALMOST FORGOT! I FINISHED MY DOCUMENTARIES ON ST. MARK'S CHURCH AND SPOOKSVILLE BEFORE I LEFT CAMP. GOT ALL INSPIRED. PASSWORD IS FORTUNATO. CHECK 'EM OUT.</u>

THE WHITE CASTLE COMMENT ELUDES ME, SINCE I'VE NEVER BEEN. APPARENTLY, THEY MAKE TINY BURGERS THAT COST, LIKE, FIVE CENTS. THAT GIRL HAS

GOT TO GET OFF THE ROAD. HER IDEA OF GOOD EATS IS GETTING SKETCHY.

She'll be at St. Mark's Church all by herself before the sun comes up and into the Spooksville Triangle soon after that. Better check out these documentaries so I know exactly what she's getting herself into.

SARAHFINCHER.COM
Password:
FORTUNATO

CLOSE CALL!

My dad just barged right in on his way to bed, acting all weird. I think Mom told him about me talking to Sarah on the phone. Not good. I barely had time to shut my laptop before he came in, and I'm sure he suspected something. I have to be more careful.

It was a long day and I'm tired, but those two videos woke me up. I still can't believe Sarah keeps going into these places all alone. She's fearless, that girl. And reckless.

A couple of things I hadn't thought of that now strike me as problems. For one thing, how the heck is she going to get inside St. Mark's Church? It'll be locked at 3:00 a.m. for sure. Check out that video and you'll see for yourself: It's not like she's going to walk right in there in the middle of the night. The Ghost Room is upstairs, in the tower, so she'll need to get inside. Something tells me she's already thought this through and her answer isn't going to be a good one.

Also, the Spooksville documentary didn't make any mention of a house or a barn out there. According to the puzzle, there should be something hidden at the hideout for B and C. . . . I sort of neglected to recall we never really figured that part out. I assumed it would figure itself out once she got there, but now that we're getting closer to the location, I'm nervous this mysterious building isn't even there. Maybe it's burned to the ground or disappeared into a sinkhole, right along with a secret message from the Apostle.

Looks like I've got plenty of work to do while Sarah drives across Utah.

If I fall asleep she'll never forgive me.

Must.

Stay.

Awake.

I'm always better at sleuthing in the middle of the night. There's less pressure and my senses are on red alert. I'm not sure if it's me worrying that someone is going to come smashing through my window or what, but I do go into a different mode after midnight.

I figured out the final location, the one marked 3. Darn proud of myself on this one. I might even have to pat myself on the back a couple of times.

Many drawings to share, so here goes.

To recap what we already know, in case we're gone and someone needs to piece this thing together . . .

Location number 1 is in Cheyenne, Wyoming. It's the St. Mark's Church, where Sarah will arrive in less than two hours.

Side 1 of the puzzle was a tower with a skeleton lying inside.

SIDE 2 WAS THE GHOST ROOM FLOOR WITH
THE MARKER, WHERE SARAH WILL NEED TO PRY UP THE
FLOORBOARD OR SOMETHING.

OKAY, SO WE'RE GOOD TO GO ON ONE OF THE CLUES. NOT SURE HOW SARAH IS GETTING IN THERE, BUT IF SHE DOES, HOPEFULLY WE'LL GET ANOTHER MESSAGE FROM THE APOSTLE.

SARAH FIGURED OUT THE SECOND DRAWING, WHICH LOOKS LIKE THIS:

THREE ROADS, THE LANTERN, THE SKELETON HAND — IT ALL LED TO THE SPOOKSVILLE TRIANGLE. AND THE RELATED PIECE FROM THE OTHER SIDE OF THE RAVEN:

THIS DRAWING MAKES IT CLEAR THAT SARAH WILL
NEED TO PARK RIGHT BELOW THE RISE IN THE ROAD,
FROM WHICH WE HOPE WE'LL FIGURE OUT WHAT THE
HIDEOUT FOR B AND C IS.

SKIPPING AHEAD TO THE FOURTH LOCATION, IT WAS
A GIMME WITH THE NICKEL — MONTICELLO, WHERE
THOMAS JEFFERSON HAD LIVED.

THE TWO PUZZLE PIECES FOR THAT ONE LOOK
LIKE THIS:

4.

Flip me over

Put the
Letters Here!

D.

CLEARLY, IT'S THE MONTICELLO BUILDING FROM
THE TAILS' SIDE OF A NICKEL, BUT WE'RE A LITTLE
STUMPED ON WHAT THE REST OF IT MEANS. PUT
THE LETTERS HERE? I KNOW WHERE WE'LL GET THE

LETTERS: FROM THE A-POSTLE VIDEOS AT THE
LOCATIONS, LIKE BEFORE. AND WE'LL PLACE THEM IN
THE RIGHT ORDER USING THE PLACES PROVIDED ON THE
RAVEN PUZZLE:

WHEN WE HAVE THE LETTERS AND WE PUT THEM IN
ORDER ON THE FRONT OF MONTICELLO, THIS WILL ALL
MAKE SENSE.

I HOPE.

SO NOW THE GOOD NEWS — THERE WAS ONE MORE
LOCATION TO FIGURE OUT AND IT HAD US BOTH STUMPED.
I FIGURED WE WERE BEING TAKEN BACK ACROSS THE

COUNTRY, SO I HAD A PRETTY GOOD IDEA THE
LOCATION WOULD BE SOMEWHERE BETWEEN MISSOURI
AND VIRGINIA. HERE'S A MAP I DREW WITH SOME OF
THE THINGS WE ALREADY KNEW AND THE AREA I
FIGURED I'D FIND THE LAST LOCATION:

SARAH'S ROAD TRIP

1	1103 miles	16 hours
2	798 miles	11.5 hours
3	980 miles	16 hours
4	537 miles	8.5 hours
5	160 miles	3 hours
6	407 miles	7.5 hours

FOLLOW THE TRAIL OF THE APOSTLE.
HE WAS HEADING BACK TO WHERE IT ALL BEGAN,
BACK TO THE PLACE WHERE THE CROSSBONES WAS
BORN ALONG WITH THE UNITED STATES OF AMERICA.
THE LOCATION HAD TO BE IN THAT BOTTOM RIGHT
CORNER OF THE UNITED STATES. I SEARCHED ALL

THROUGH TENNESSEE, KENTUCKY, NORTH AND SOUTH CAROLINA, ALABAMA, AND MISSISSIPPI FOR HAUNTED PLACES STARTING WITH THE LETTERS S AND G UNTIL ABOUT A HALF HOUR AGO, I LITERALLY SLAPPED MYSELF IN THE FOREHEAD.

So STUPID!

HERE'S THE DRAWING FROM THE RAVEN PUZZLE:

WHY DID IT TAKE ME SO LONG TO FIGURE THIS OUT?

THE G IS FOR GEORGIA, WHICH IS RIGHT IN LINE

WITH A TRIP ACROSS THE COUNTRY. AND IF THE G WAS FOR GEORGIA, THEN THE S WAS FOR A CITY. A CITY WHERE A FIRE TOOK PLACE. A BIG ONE.

AS IT TURNS OUT, WITHOUT MUCH INVESTIGATING AT ALL, I FOUND THE FIRE.

SAVANNAH, GEORGIA. THE FIRE OF 1820, A FIRE THAT ENGULFED TWO-THIRDS OF THE CITY. I COULDN'T HELP THINKING SKELETON CREEK HAD SURVIVED A FIRE JUST LIKE IT IN ITS OWN PAST.

COINCIDENCE?

HARDLY!

TWO HUGE FIRES IN TWO CROSSBONES STRONGHOLDS? I THINK THEY HAD SOMETHING TO DO WITH IT. THEY BURNED JEFFERSON'S HOUSE DOWN. THESE GUYS ARE KNOWN PYROMANIACS.

THE DOWN ARROW AND THE NUMBER 30 GOT ME TO THE LOCATION. TAKE 30 AWAY FROM 1820 AND YOU GET 1790.

THE 17 HUNDRED 90 BUILDING, A HAUNTED HOTEL IN A HAUNTED CITY. AND THE MOST HAUNTED ROOM IN THAT HOTEL? LOOK NO FURTHER THAN THE CLUE ON THE OTHER SIDE OF THE PUZZLE.

ROOM 204. A ROOM YOU CAN STILL STAY IN
TODAY. IF YOU'RE CRAZY!

I DON'T THINK SARAH IS CRAZY, BUT I DO THINK
SHE'S MORE THAN WILLING TO STAY IN A HAUNTED
HOTEL ROOM IF IT GETS US SOME ANSWERS WE NEED.
THAT'S A NO-BRAINER.

I'M GOING TO TAKE A QUICK BREAK, FINISH DRAWING
THIS MAP, SCAN IT, AND SEND IT TO SARAH. THAT WAY
SHE'LL HAVE A VISUAL. AND I'M GRABBING A BOWL OF
CHEERIOS WITH A TON OF SUGAR. I'M CRASHING!

BACK IN A SEC.

SATURDAY, JULY 16, 2:00 A.M.

FINISHED THE RAVEN MAP AND SENT IT TO SARAH.
WE'RE ALL DIALED IN. ALSO SLAMMED SOME SUGARY
CEREAL, SO I SHOULD BE ABLE TO STAY AWAKE FOR AT
LEAST ANOTHER HOUR.

    HERE'S THE FINALIZED MAP, THE JOURNEY BACK
AGAIN, FOLLOWING THE TRAIL OF THE A-POSTLE:

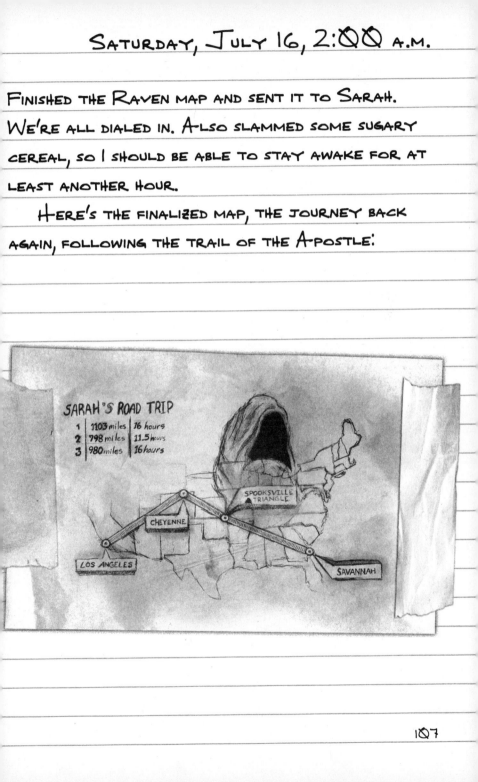

THE COOL THING IS THAT IT ENDS ON THE SAME COAST AS BOSTON, WHERE SARAH LIVES. SHE WON'T EVEN HAVE TO GO THAT FAR OUT OF HER WAY IN ORDER TO MAKE ALL THE STOPS. THAT'LL HELP WITH KEEPING HER PARENTS CALM EVEN IF SHE IS VISITING HAUNTED LOCATIONS.

I'M GOING TO PRINT OUT MY EMAIL TO SARAH AND PUT IT HERE IN MY JOURNAL.

I WISH I COULD STOP YAWNING!

COME ON, DUDE, YOU CAN DO THIS. ONE MORE HOUR. STAY AWAKE.

Sarah,

I hope you're able to get this email on your phone when you stop in the middle of the night. If so, just know I'm here for you. I'm awake and waiting for your call. We didn't have a chance to cover how you'll get in there, but maybe you've got that figured out. Don't do anything too wild, okay?

I figured out the final location tonight. Figuring out locations isn't driving across Utah drinking Lime Rickeys and eating fry sauce, but still — I'm pretty awesome! I won't bore you with the details of how I solved it, but you should know the backstory of the place if you're going in there. I know, I know, you'll do your own research and make a killer documentary, squashing my contribution like a bug. I'll bask in my moment, however short it will be.

(Insert game show voice here) — You'll be traveling to sunny Savannah, Georgia, staying at the swanky 17 Hundred 90 Hotel. We'll even book you in the most haunted room they've got: room 204!

Okay, enough shenanigans, here's the scoop:

At one time, the hotel was a boardinghouse, where a sixteen-year-old girl used to live. (Maybe it was you in a past life! Wouldn't that be something?) Her name was Anna Powell and she was kind of naive. She fell in love with a visiting sailor, who promptly took off for the high seas, promising to return soon and marry her. Months went by. No letters, no sailor. Soon everyone agreed: He was probably married and never intended to return to a heartsick girl in Savannah. Maybe he would have returned if he'd known how distraught Anna Powell would become. One night, her heart broken to pieces, she threw herself off the balcony of the hotel to the bricks below.

Ew.

The room she jumped from? 204, the same number that resides on the Raven Puzzle. The same room you'll be staying in if we're going to find what the Apostle hid there. You'll recall there were wisps of air all around the number 204, which makes me think you'll want to search in the air vents. I bet that's where you'll find what we're looking for.

Oh, just so you know, that room is SO haunted. But we can talk about that later.

Call me!

Ryan

THERE, GOT THAT ALL IN HERE FOR POSTERITY. IF NOTHING ELSE, IT SHOWS THAT I FIGURED THIS PART OUT.

I THINK I'LL TAKE A BREAK. JUST SIT HERE AT MY DESK. MAYBE PLAY A VIDEO GAME.

SATURDAY, JULY 16, 6:10 A.M.

I TOLD MYSELF ABOUT A THOUSAND TIMES THAT I WOULDN'T LET THIS HAPPEN. I DID PUSH-UPS. I DRANK HIGHLY CAFFEINATED BEVERAGES. I PULLED HAIRS OUT OF MY ARM. BUT IT HAPPENED ANYWAY.

I FELL ASLEEP.

NOT JUST A LITTLE, EITHER. I CONKED OUT BIG-TIME. THREE HOURS!

I AM HOPELESSLY LAME.

THERE IS ONE PIECE OF GOOD NEWS. OR MAYBE IT'S TERRIBLE NEWS. YEAH, IT'S TERRIBLE NEWS. I CHECKED MY PHONE AND SARAH NEVER CALLED ME. I MEAN, IT SUGGESTS THAT SHE DOESN'T KNOW I FELL ASLEEP, SO THERE'S THAT. BUT IT ALSO MEANS SHE'S GONE MISSING. I'LL TAKE MAD SARAH OVER MISSING SARAH ANY DAY OF THE WEEK.

RING!!!

SATURDAY, JULY 16, 6:30 A.M.

GREAT NEWS ON SO MANY FRONTS! THAT PHONE RING I SHOVED IN THERE AT THE END OF MY LAST ENTRY? IT WAS SARAH. APPARENTLY, WYOMING HAS SOME HUMONGOUS CELL PHONE DEAD ZONES. SHE COULDN'T GET A SIGNAL, WHICH IS WHY SHE DIDN'T CALL ME FROM ST. MARK'S CHURCH. I FEEL SLIGHTLY CONFLICTED ABOUT NOT MENTIONING THE WHOLE FALLING-ASLEEP THING, BUT SHE DIDN'T ASK AND I DIDN'T TELL.

THERE'S MORE.

SARAH PULLED IN LATE, ABOUT 4:00 A.M., AND PARKED ON A SIDE STREET. THEN SHE GOT HER CAMERA OUT AND STARTED FILMING EVERYTHING. THE SUN WAS ABOUT AN HOUR FROM COMING UP, SO THE CHURCH PARKING LOT WAS EMPTY AND NO ONE WAS AROUND. SOMEWHAT SURPRISINGLY, SHE HAD NO PLAN ONCE SHE FIGURED OUT ALL THE DOORS WERE LOCKED. ALL SHE HAD WAS A PHILLIPS SCREWDRIVER AND A PRAYER. SHE WAS COMPELLED TO SHARE THE PRAYER WITH ME:

PLEASE GOD, SHOW ME A WAY IN. WE JUST WANT TO FIGURE THIS OUT. AND I'D LIKE TO GET SOME SLEEP. I'M LIKE THE WALKING DEAD. AMEN.

A quick walk around the entire building yielded no better results. She was still locked out, and very soon the sun would be up over Wyoming. By 4:30 a.m., she was back in her car, discouraged and bleary-eyed. She thought seriously about heading for the hotel and crashing. No cell signal, no way in. A total waste of a thousand miles on the road.

How depressing.

And then poof! Just like that, her prayer was answered. A car pulled into the church parking lot at 4:45 a.m. An old guy stepped out of the car. He meandered, whistling an early morning tune, then unlocked the front door and went inside. Sarah stayed put as two more cars pulled up. It was like a crack-of-dawn convention at St. Mark's, and Sarah's spirits started to brighten.

"From the looks of it, this was some sort of early-bird-catches-the-worm Bible study," Sarah told me. "So I figured once they were all inside, the door would still be unlocked and I could sneak up into the tower."

She figured right. Really old people get up very early. It's like a curse or something. A few minutes later, as the sun was starting to rise, she crept through the morning shadows and into the church. Then she turned her camera on. Even I could hear the echo of voices and laughter drifting down a hallway as she turned and started walking. I could practically see the Styrofoam coffee cups, the folding metal chairs, and three old-timers gathered in a circle. She checked a couple of doors, both locked, then came to a stairway leading up.

"I knew the Ghost Room was upstairs, near the bell, so I just started hoofing it as quietly and as fast as I could," she explained, breathless with excitement. "The stairwell was dark, just a little light creeping in from the windows at the very top. About halfway up, there was a landing and an old door."

The door wasn't even shut all the way. It was open just a crack, and pushing it, the hinges creaked down the staircase. She stood stock-still, peering into the room, hoping no one had

HEARD THE SOUND. THE OPENING WAS BARELY BIG ENOUGH FOR SARAH TO FIT THROUGH IF SHE TURNED SIDEWAYS, AND ONCE SHE WAS INSIDE, THE NOISES PERSISTED. SHE FOUND HERSELF STANDING ON CREAKING FLOORBOARDS.

"TALK ABOUT A NOISY CHURCH," SHE CONCLUDED. "HAD TO BE ALL THREE OLD GUYS WERE HARD OF HEARING. BETWEEN THE DOOR AND THE FLOOR, I WAS MAKING QUITE A RACKET."

SHE SET THE CAMERA DOWN, FOUND THE FLOORBOARD SHE WAS SUPPOSED TO PULL UP, AND WENT TO WORK. SHE SAID THIS WAS THE LOUDEST THING SO FAR. NOTHING LIKE PRYING UP A PIECE OF FLOORING TO WAKE THE DEAD, BUT SHE WORKED QUICKLY AND NO ONE SEEMED TO TAKE ANY NOTICE OF WHAT SHE WAS DOING.

THEN SARAH HEARD SHUFFLING FOOTSTEPS COMING UP THE NARROW STAIRWAY.

WHAT HAPPENED NEXT SHE WOULDN'T SAY, BUT SHE GOT WHAT SHE'D COME FOR: UNDER THE FLOORBOARD, REACHING HER HAND INSIDE, A REEL OF FILM. THE APOSTLE WAS ABOUT TO SPEAK TO US ONCE MORE.

BUT THE APOSTLE WASN'T THE ONLY ONE WITH A MESSAGE FOR US.

No, it was far worse then that.

The ghost of Old Joe Bush had come up the stairs.

He'd paused outside the door, pushed it in a tad, then stopped.

Silence.

Followed by what?

Sarah hung up after that. She wanted to show me everything that had happened and thought she'd need about an hour to put together the footage. She had the ancient 8mm projector with her, which she'd brought up to her room, so converting the Apostle message to video would be quick. She'd do like she had before, projecting the old footage onto a white sheet while she videotaped it.

And she was going to send me a copy of her adventure at St. Mark's Church.

I know my dad will expect me out the door by 7:45 a.m. It's Saturday, our busiest day of the week.

Come on, Sarah, send me something. I've only got twenty or so minutes. After that I'll be locked in the shop all day, where it might be too busy to sneak a look online.

The thought of not seeing what she found is killing me. I don't think I can go all day without knowing.

Man, she must be tired. Maybe she fell asleep.

MY DAD JUST CALLED ME DOWNSTAIRS, BUT I FINALLY
GOT AN EMAIL FROM SARAH. I YELLED DOWN THE
STAIRS, TOLD MY DAD I'D BE RIGHT DOWN, AND READ
HER NOTE.

Ryan,

I'm barely awake right now, so this is going to be superfast. Seeing the
ghost of Old Joe Bush just about fried my brain. And the Apostle video
is vintage weirdness, as expected. I posted both videos at the site and
used osiris as the password.

The strangest part about what just happened?

I'm not afraid of Old Joe Bush anymore.

Me go sleep now.

S.

P.S. What's the clause? You holding out on me?

P.P.S. At the end of the video, be ready for a jolt when you look up.
That's my only warning.

SARAHFINCHER.COM
Password:
OSIRIS

SATURDAY, JULY 16, 7:45 A.M.

OSIRIS: GOD OF DEATH AND THE UNDERWORLD. VERY NICE.

IF YOU ASK ME, WHATEVER FOUND SARAH IN ST. MARK'S CHURCH IS JUST AS SCARY AS EVER. AND SHE'S RIGHT ABOUT THE APOSTLE — THAT GUY IS SO OUT THERE. WATCHING HIM NEVER GETS OLD.

BUT THERE WAS SOMETHING ELSE, SOMETHING I HAVE TO CONTACT HER ABOUT. SARAH DIDN'T JUST FIND A REEL OF OLD FILM UNDER THE FLOORBOARDS IN THE GHOST ROOM. SHE FOUND A GLASS VIAL OF LIQUID, TOO. AND DO YOU KNOW WHAT WAS SCRAWLED ON THE LABEL? TWO WORDS.

THE CLAUSE.

AND BELOW THOSE TWO WORDS, FOUR MORE:

WHEN THERE IS ONE.

DAD JUST YELLED UP AGAIN. BETTER NOT LET HIM COME UP HERE.

SATURDAY, JULY 16, 3:00 P.M.

MY DAD LET ME OFF EARLY AFTER I BEGGED FOR SOME TIME ON THE RIVER. I DON'T REALLY WANT TO GO FISHING, BUT IT'S A GOOD COVER FOR WHAT I NEED TO DO.

FIRST A FEW NOTES, THEN I'M GETTING ON MY MOUNTAIN BIKE AND HEADING DOWNSTREAM.

I NEED TO GET A MESSAGE TO FITZ, AND THE ONLY WAY THAT'S GOING TO HAPPEN IS AT THE BIG TREE IN THE CLEARING.

OKAY, SO A FEW NOTES BEFORE I GO.

1) I DON'T AGREE WITH SARAH ABOUT THE GHOST OF OLD JOE BUSH. SOMETHING SEEMED WRONG THIS TIME, FOR SURE, LIKE HENRY OR POSSESSED HENRY OR WHOEVER WAS HAVING SOME TROUBLE BREATHING. BUT THAT DOESN'T MAKE HIM ANY LESS DANGEROUS. AND SEEING HIM REACH DOWN AT HER LIKE THAT REALLY BOTHERED ME. STILL, I WASN'T THERE, SO I DON'T KNOW WHAT IT FELT LIKE. SARAH SEEMS TO THINK WE SHOULDN'T DO ANYTHING BUT KEEP GOING. EITHER HER NERVES HAVE

TURNED TO STEEL OR SHE'S LOST HER MARBLES, BECAUSE THAT DUDE IS EVERY BIT AS HAIR-RAISING AS HE EVER WAS, IF YOU ASK ME. IT IS STRANGE, THOUGH, HOW HE NEVER SEEMS TO COME AFTER US. HE SEEMS TO BE WATCHING US, MAYBE EVEN TRYING TO HELP. ODD. I'LL ADMIT THERE IS A BIG PART OF ME THAT FEELS BAD ABOUT NOT TELLING MY DAD WE'RE SEEING HIS OLD BUDDY HENRY OUT IN THE WORLD ACTING LIKE HE'S COMPLETELY LOST IT. AND THERE'S THE FACT THAT, TECHNICALLY, HE'S A FUGITIVE. WHEN I THINK ABOUT THINGS LIKE THAT, I WONDER HOW IN THE WORLD WE EVER GOT IN SO DEEP. IT'S LIKE WE'VE FALLEN UNDER A SPELL AND WE CAN'T WAKE UP UNTIL WE REACH THE END.

2) I HAVE TO CALL SARAH AND LEAVE HER A MESSAGE. SHE'LL BE SLEEPING FOR ANOTHER HOUR OR TWO, BUT SHE NEEDS TO SEND ME THAT VIAL OF LIQUID. SHE'S OUT WEST, SO IF SHE CAN JUST GET IT IN THE OVERNIGHT MAIL BEFORE SHE LEAVES, IT SHOULD ARRIVE ON MONDAY. I HAVE A FEELING I KNOW WHAT IT'S

FOR, BUT I CAN'T SAY FOR SURE. EITHER WAY, THAT VIAL OF LIQUID NEEDS TO MAKE ITS WAY TO SKELETON CREEK PRONTO.

3) THE A-POSTLE VIDEO PROVIDED US WITH THE FIRST OF THREE LETTERS WE'RE SEARCHING FOR. NO WORDS ON THE CARDS THIS TIME AROUND, JUST SINGLE LETTERS. THE FIRST IS AN A. SO NOW THE RAVEN PUZZLE LOOKS LIKE THIS:

4) It's a little unnerving seeing that secret book in the Apostle's hand. The fact that the very same book is now in my backpack makes me feel like I've got a bull's-eye on my back with the shape of a Raven's head. He knows I have it. I can feel it. It's only a matter of time before he comes looking for it.

Phone call to Sarah made, told her to overnight the vial today — check.
Note to Fitz written — check.
Patch kit packed — check (there are a billion ways to get a flat tire on the river trail).

Ready to roll.
Here's hoping I make it back before dark without any unexpected encounters with the Raven.

MY SENSE OF DIRECTION IS WACKED WHEN I GET ON THE RIVER. LET'S BE HONEST: I HAVE NO SENSE OF DIRECTION. <u>EVER.</u> YOU'D THINK I'D KNOW THE WILDERNESS LIKE THE BACK OF MY HAND, BUT IT'S ALWAYS BEEN A WEAKNESS OF MINE. I THINK YOU'RE EITHER BORN WITH A SENSE OF DIRECTION OR YOU'RE NOT. FOR ME, NORTH, EAST, SOUTH, AND WEST ARE LIKE A FOREIGN LANGUAGE. IF SOMEONE WALKED UP TO ME RIGHT NOW AND SAID, "POINT NORTH," I'D SAY, "YOU MEAN LEFT, RIGHT, OR TOWARD THE MOON? GIVE ME A CLUE HERE." I'M THAT BAD. IN FACT, WHEN I GET OLD, LIKE FIFTY, THEY'LL SERIOUSLY NEED TO TAKE AWAY MY CAR KEYS. I'LL BE JUST THE KIND OF GEEZER THAT WILL DRIVE OUT INTO THE COUNTRY AND END UP ON A DIRT ROAD IN NEVADA BY SUNRISE.

ANYWAY, THE POINT OF ALL THAT IS TO SAY, WOW, IT TOOK ME PRACTICALLY FOREVER TO FIND THAT STUPID TREE AGAIN. I ABANDONED MY BIKE AND WADED ACROSS THE RIVER, WHICH IS RUNNING ABOUT THREE FEET DEEP AT ITS HIGHEST RIGHT NOW. THE ENTIRE TIME I KEPT REPEATING TO MYSELF, <u>WHY DID YOU BRING THE GHOST BOOK WITH YOU?</u> DON'T SLIP

AND FALL IN THE WATER, YOU IDIOT! WHICH WAY IS SOUTH?

FROM THE TIME I CROSSED THE RIVER, TO THE MOMENT I FOUND THE CLEARING WITH THE MONSTER TREE, AT LEAST TWO HOURS PASSED. THEN I GOT SO NERVOUS ABOUT CROSSING THE OPEN SPACE ALONE. I STOOD IN THE TREES FOR ANOTHER TWENTY MINUTES TRYING TO GET MY NERVE UP. I HAD A STRONG FEELING THE RAVEN, HOODED AND CARRYING THAT OUTRAGEOUS AX, WAS GOING TO COME RUNNING DOWN THE RAVINE AND CHASE ME THROUGH THE WOODS.

WHEN I FINALLY DID GET TO THE TREE, I FOUND THE PLACE WHERE THE RAVEN HAD BEEN CHOPPING. IT WAS A NICE BIG DIVOT, AND TO MY SURPRISE, THERE WAS ALREADY A NOTE IN THERE. I WAS BEYOND FREAKED OUT STANDING IN THE OPEN, LIKE I WAS IN THE MIDDLE OF THE SCHOOL CAFETERIA WEARING NOTHING BUT MY UNDERWEAR. SO INSTEAD OF READING THE NOTE LIKE A NORMAL PERSON, I GRABBED IT, STUFFED MY LETTER TO FITZ INTO THE TREE, AND RAN LIKE A MANIAC. I DON'T THINK I SCREAMED WHILE I RAN, BUT I SORT OF BLACKED OUT DURING THE WHOLE RUNNING-AWAY THING, SO I MIGHT HAVE. I DIDN'T STOP UNTIL I GOT TO THE RIVER,

WHERE I REALIZED HOW OVERHEATED AND THIRSTY I WAS. AN HOUR OF RUNNING THROUGH THE WOODS WILL DO THAT TO A GUY. THAT, AND I HAD ABOUT A THOUSAND SCRATCHES AND BRUISES FROM HEAD TO TOE FROM BUSHES AND LOW-HANGING BRANCHES. THOSE THINGS STING WHEN YOU CROSS A RIVER.

NOW I'M SITTING HERE WRITING ALL THIS DOWN BECAUSE, SERIOUSLY, I'M EXHAUSTED. I NEED A BREAK OR I'LL NEVER MAKE IT OUT ALIVE.

WHEN I GOT TO THE OTHER SIDE OF THE RIVER, I FELT BETTER, LIKE I WAS OUT OF THE RAVEN'S DOMAIN AND HE COULDN'T TOUCH ME ANYMORE. STILL, THERE'S REALLY NO REASON FOR ME TO FEEL COMFORTED BECAUSE THE RIVER IS BETWEEN ME AND THE GIANT TREE. BUT FOR SOME REASON I DO FEEL CALMER NOW THAT THE TASK IS DONE.

FOUR HOURS. THAT'S HOW LONG IT TOOK ME TO GET A NOTE TO FITZ, AND I'M STILL NOT OUT OF THE WOODS YET. ON A GOOD DAY, WHEN I'M NOT TOTALLY WINDED, IT TAKES ME AN HOUR AND A HALF TO RIDE BACK UP THE TRAIL FROM HERE TO SKELETON CREEK. BUT SITTING HERE BY MY BIKE, I CAN TELL IT'S GOING TO TAKE ME A LOT LONGER. THE SUN IS ALREADY OFF

THE WATER AND I'M — WHAT? AN HOUR FROM
SUNSET?

NOT A GOOD SITUATION.

I SHOULD BE UP AND MOVING, BUT I JUST FINISHED A
HARROWING FOUR-HOUR JOURNEY AND MY MUSCLES
ARE CRAMPING UP. JUST A LITTLE MORE REST.

HERE'S WHAT FITZ WROTE TO ME:

Ryan,
    If you get this, you should know my dad's been talking
about moving on. He says there's no reason to stay here
much longer. He keeps talking about one more thing he has
to do, but he won't say what it is.
    I hope it doesn't have anything to do with you.
    I also hope I get to see you again, but I have a
feeling this is good-bye.
    Your friend,
    Fitz

SORT OF A SAD NOTE. I FEEL BAD FOR FITZ.

MY NOTE TO HIM (I MADE A COPY BEFORE I LEFT
IT IN THE TREE):

Fitz,

Sarah found a vial of some sort of liquid. She's mailing it to me and I should have it Monday. I think it might be useful on "the clause," but I don't know for sure. My guess? That thing has some sort of invisible ink and whatever is in this vial will unlock it. Besides "the clause," the vial had four other words on it: "when there is one." Confusing. Does it mean "when there's a clause, the vial comes into play" or does it mean something totally different, like "when there's a number one"? Typical Crossbones doublespeak.

I'm going to leave the vial at your old trailer under the front steps. Whoever owns it hasn't rented it out again, so it's vacant. Come into town and get it late Monday night if you can.

I HOPE YOU'VE GOT SOMETHING TO READ UP THERE. MUST BE BORING.

RYAN

8:26 P.M. NO MORE MR. LAZY. I GOTTA GET THE HECK OUT OF THESE WOODS AND FAST.

TIME TO RIDE.

SATURDAY, JULY 16, 9:05 P.M.

SUN IS JUST ABOUT DOWN AND I'M SO TIRED I CAN BARELY MOVE MY LEGS. A GOOD HOUR TO GO. I USED A BUNGEE CORD TO ATTACH MY FLASHLIGHT TO THE HANDLEBARS SO I CAN SEE THE TRAIL. I HAVE THIS AWFUL FEELING I'M BEING FOLLOWED, AND WHATEVER IS FOLLOWING ME IS JUST WAITING FOR DARKNESS TO SETTLE IN. IT'S LOUD ON MY BIKE — THE SOUND OF THE WHEELS ON DIRT AND ROCKS — SO I KEEP STOPPING, LISTENING FOR SOMETHING BEHIND ME.

ONE THING I DIDN'T WRITE DOWN BEFORE THAT I SHOULD NOW. IT'S WHAT GOT ME ON MY BIKE, PEDDLING LIKE THE WIND.

ACROSS THE RIVER, STANDING ON THE SHORE.

THE RAVEN WAS WATCHING ME.

I'M ONE FLAT TIRE FROM NOT MAKING IT OUT OF THE WOODS ALIVE.

SATURDAY, JULY 16, 11:25 P.M.

Is it really 11:25 P.M.? How did that happen? How did I lose an entire afternoon and night delivering a note?

About a half hour after my last entry, I bumped into my dad coming down the trail. Scared me so bad I nearly rode right into a tree. He was relieved to find me, to say the least. All I can say is I'm glad I brought my fly box and a pack rod with me, or I'd have had zero alibi for why I was out on the trail so late. As it was, I covered pretty good.

"Your mother is worried sick," he started in. "And the mayor is about to send for the National Guard. What were you thinking?"

I went on and on about how amazing the fishing was — beyond any day I'd ever fished in my life, how I'd completely lost track of time. How sorry I was.

I felt about as small as an ant. I hated lying to him like that, but even more, I knew it was a lie I would get away with. I was using his weakness against him.

132

"That good, huh?" he said, a twinkle in his eye. He was already halfway to forgiving me, staring into the dark in the direction of the water.

Then I did the unthinkable. I held my arms out as if I were showing the size of the biggest one I'd caught, about two feet long.

"No way," he said.

I just nodded, smiled weakly, and started walking my bike next to him.

"What'd you catch him on? How long did it take to reel him in? Rainbow or brown trout?"

We talked about the mythical whale fish all the way back home as I kept feeling worse and worse. I'd promised myself I wouldn't keep telling whoppers, and there I was telling a fish story the size of Texas.

My dad smoothed things over with my mom, but she was so happy to see me it didn't take much. And the mayor, who had staked out our front porch, was so relieved he hugged me.

Yuck.

A shower, some Band-Aids, and a plate of potato salad have given me a second wind I didn't

EXPECT. ALL NIGHT LONG, I'VE BEEN THINKING OF SARAH AND HOW SHE MUST BE TRYING TO CONTACT ME. BACK IN CELL RANGE, I'D FOUND A STRING OF THREE TEXT MESSAGES. SHE'D ALSO TRIED CALLING TWICE, BUT HADN'T LEFT A MESSAGE.

4:06 P.M.
YOU DIDN'T PICK UP, SO YOU MUST STILL BE WORKING. I'M ON THE ROAD. LOOKS LIKE 1:00 A.M. AT SPOOKSVILLE IF I'M LUCKY.

8:57 P.M.
PASSING THROUGH KANSAS. FLAT. BORED. WHERE ARE YOU?

10:29 P.M.
AHEAD OF SCHEDULE, SHOULD BE THERE A LITTLE AFTER MIDNIGHT. HOPEFULLY, I'LL HAVE A SIGNAL! NOT THAT YOU'LL BE THERE TO PICK UP.

AS FAR AS SARAH'S PARENTS KNEW, SHE WAS STILL SNOOZING IN CHEYENNE, WYOMING, AND WOULDN'T

LEAVE FOR THE NEXT STOP ON HER HAUNTED TOUR
UNTIL MORNING. IT WAS ALL GETTING A LITTLE HARD TO
FOLLOW FROM SKELETON CREEK, BUT I UNDERSTOOD
THE BASICS.

SARAH WAS STAYING WHERE HER PARENTS HAD
TOLD HER TO STAY, BUT DOING IT TWELVE HOURS IN
ADVANCE OF WHEN SHE WAS SUPPOSED TO DO IT. IT WAS
THIS SWITCH IN TIME THAT ALLOWED HER TO VISIT THE
HAUNTED LOCATIONS AT NIGHT, WHEN NO ONE WAS
AROUND. SHE WAS SCHEDULED TO ARRIVE AT A SUPER 8
IN JOPLIN, MISSOURI, IN ABOUT FIFTEEN HOURS, BUT
SHE'D BE THERE WAY EARLY. IT WAS A PERFECT
HALFWAY POINT, A CHANCE FOR HER TO TAKE A NICE
LONG REST BEFORE CONTINUING ON TO SAVANNAH,
WHERE HER PARENTS, AGAINST THEIR BETTER
JUDGMENT, HAD AGREED TO PAY FOR A ROOM AT THE
17 HUNDRED 90.

I TEXTED SARAH BACK, HOPING SHE WOULDN'T TRY
TO READ IT WHILE DRIVING, AND WAITED.

I WAS <u>NOT</u> FALLING ASLEEP THIS TIME. I PUT ON
SOME MUSIC, SURFED THE WEB, WAITED.

FOUR MINUTES LATER, SHE CALLED.

"RYAN! WHERE HAVE YOU BEEN?"

"DID YOU PULL OVER?" SAFETY FIRST. THE LAST THING SHE NEEDED TO BE DOING WAS DRIVING AND TALKING ON HER PHONE. IT WAS STRESSFUL ENOUGH KNOWING SHE WAS OUT THERE ALL ALONE.

"YEAH, I PULLED OVER. DON'T TRY TO CHANGE THE SUBJECT."

I EXPLAINED EVERYTHING AS FAST AS I COULD, THEN ASKED HER IF SHE'D GOTTEN MY MESSAGE AND SENT THE VIAL.

"IT'S ON THE WAY. I EVEN PAID EXTRA TO MAKE SURE IT ARRIVES ON MONDAY. YOU OWE ME."

SHE ALSO SAID SHE'D THOUGHT ABOUT PULLING AN ALICE IN WONDERLAND AND DRINKING WHATEVER WAS INSIDE, BUT WHEN SHE TWISTED THE TOP OPEN SHE'D CHANGED HER MIND.

"WOULD HAVE BEEN FUN SHRINKING DOWN TO THE SIZE OF A WATER BOTTLE, BUT WHATEVER IS IN THERE DOESN'T SMELL TOO GOOD. MORE LIKELY I'D HAVE GROWN A THIRD ARM OUT OF MY FOREHEAD."

THANKS, SARAH, NOW ALL I CAN THINK ABOUT IS

MY BEST FRIEND WITH AN ARM STICKING OUT OF HER FACE. GHASTLY.

I TOLD HER TO WATCH THE DIRECTIONS CAREFULLY, BECAUSE THERE WAS A VERY SPECIFIC PLACE SHE HAD TO PARK.

"I KNOW THE PLACE — IT'S CALLED THE MIDDLE OF NOWHERE," SHE JOKED. "CAN'T MISS IT."

SARAH LAUGHED, THEN TOLD ME SHE WAS HIGH-FIVING THE ARM STICKING OUT OF HER FOREHEAD, WHICH SHE'D NAMED JUDITH.

SHE HAD TO FOLLOW DIRECTIONS OFF THE HIGHWAY, DOWN A TWO LANE, ONTO A DIRT ROAD, AND INTO JUST THE RIGHT SPOT, WHERE THE ROAD WOULD RISE BEFORE HER.

"Hopefully, when you get there, you'll see a building shaped like the one in the picture. That'll be the hideout for B and C."

Even saying it made me scratch my head. The hideout for B and C? If this mystery doesn't solve itself, I didn't know what we're going to do.

I told Sarah about dropping the note to Fitz, and she said she'd try to call when she arrived at the Spooksville Triangle, which she guessed would be in about an hour.

Then she said she was going to let Judith drive, and hung up.

AN HOUR IS A LONG TIME WHEN YOU'VE HAD THE KIND OF DAY I JUST HAD. I'M WORRIED I'M GOING TO FALL ASLEEP AGAIN. I'M GOING TO DREAM OF THE RAVEN CHASING ME THROUGH THE WOODS. HE'S GOING TO CATCH ME, AND WHEN I FINALLY SEE INSIDE THAT DARK HOOD OF HIS, THERE WILL BE A BLACK CLAW STICKING OUT OF HIS HEAD. THE BLACK CLAW WILL GRAB MY FACE AND LIFT ME OFF THE GROUND.

OKAY, I'M WIDE AWAKE NOW. I DON'T THINK THERE'S MUCH CHANCE OF ME GETTING ANY SLEEP TONIGHT WITH A DREAM LIKE THAT WAITING FOR ME.

IT'S PAST MIDNIGHT. SHE SHOULD BE GETTING INTO POSITION.

I HAVE TO REMEMBER TO SET MY WEBCAM TO RECORD AGAIN.

I THINK I JUST FELL ASLEEP WITH MY EYES OPEN, BECAUSE MY HEAD SNAPPED BACK AND I ALMOST FELL OUT OF MY CHAIR.

COME ON, SARAH. HAVE A SIGNAL. CALL ME. SOON.

SUNDAY, JULY 17, 12:35 A.M.

It's Sunday in Skeleton Creek, dark outside my window, and the world just changed in a flash.

Everything is different now. I'm not sure if I'm sad, relieved, worried, or scared. Maybe I'm all those things at once.

I'm going to relay this exactly as it happened, because there's a real possibility I'll be asked about it someday. I want to make sure I have it written down exactly as it occurred.

Sarah called me from the Spooksville Triangle at 12:27 a.m. She was parked right where she needed to be, where the desolate road rose in front of her.

"It's freakin' <u>dark</u> out here, Ryan," she said. "If I turn off my headlights it's pitch-black. How am I supposed to find a building if I can't see it?"

I thought about this for a second, then asked her if she had a flashlight.

"Of course I have a flashlight. I'm a girl alone in the dark!"

Right, of course she has a flashlight. So I asked her how she felt about getting out of the

CAR AND POINTING THE LIGHT ALONG THE SIDES OF THE ROAD.

"DID I MENTION THE PART ABOUT IT BEING PITCH-BLACK AND TOTALLY SPOOKY OUT HERE?"

"YOU DID."

I WANTED TO TELL HER I'D RIDDEN MY MOUNTAIN BIKE AT NIGHT INTO THE LAIR OF THE RAVEN. I WANTED TO TELL HER ABOUT THE CLAW DREAM I'D IMAGINED, ABOUT THE GROVE AND THE TREE AND ALL THE TERRIBLE, SCARY THINGS IN MY LIFE. BUT WHAT GOOD WAS THAT GOING TO DO? SHE HAD HER OWN FEARS TO FACE, AND TELLING HER ABOUT MINE WOULDN'T SOLVE ANYTHING.

AND THAT'S WHEN IT HAPPENED.

THAT'S WHEN MY OLD WORLD CAME TO AN END AND A NEW WORLD BEGAN.

"RYAN?" SARAH WHISPERED. "DON'T YOU DARE HANG UP."

"I WON'T."

"YOU KNOW THAT LEGEND ABOUT THE LIGHT THAT PEOPLE SEE DANCING OVER THE RISE IN THE ROAD?"

"I DO. IT'S THE LADY WITH THE LAMP, LOOKING FOR HER LOST KID. WHY DO YOU ASK?"

141

"Because I just turned my headlights on. I don't see a light. I see something else."

"What do you see?"

There was a long pause as Sarah reached around and locked all the doors.

"What's going on, Sarah? Talk to me!"

"He's coming down the road."

I wanted to ask her who. But that would have been stupid. I knew who it was without her having to say.

"Get out of there! Just drive!" I yelled.

"I can't move, Ryan. He's coming for me. He's coming down the hill on that shattered leg of his."

I yelled for her to start the car and drive, then realized how stupid yelling was. What if my parents heard me? It was after midnight and they were both sound sleepers. There was my door — closed — and their door, also closed. But I'd yelled pretty loudly.

"I'm getting out of the car," Sarah said. "Don't worry. It's all going to be okay."

I WAS ON THE VERGE OF A TOTAL MELTDOWN, WHISPERING AS LOUDLY AS I FELT I COULD, "GET BACK IN THE CAR! GET OUT OF THERE!"

I HEARD THE DOOR OPEN AND SHUT. I HEARD FOOTSTEPS ON A DIRT ROAD.

SARAH? WHAT'S HAPPENING? SARAH!

WAS SHE POSSESSED? HAD SHE GONE INSANE WITH FEAR?

"RYAN," SHE WHISPERED.

"YEAH?" MY VOICE WAS TREMBLING. I WAS SURE HENRY OR THE GHOST OR WHATEVER HAD FOLLOWED MY FRIEND HALFWAY ACROSS THE COUNTRY HAD FINALLY GOTTEN HER.

BUT THEN SHE SAID SOMETHING I DIDN'T EXPECT.

"THE GHOST OF OLD JOE BUSH JUST DIED IN MY ARMS."

SUNDAY, JULY 17, 1:25 A.M.

It's funny how the mind works. An hour ago I was so tired I could barely keep my eyes open. Now I feel like I've downed five cups of coffee with a Red Bull chaser.

Henry is dead.

I had to write that down, just once, to make it real.

And if Henry is dead, then so is the ghost of Old Joe Bush. There was never one without the other, and now both are laid to rest.

Sarah videotaped the entire encounter, which she says was one of the most harrowing experiences of her life. Seeing him in the beams of her headlights, his figure coming up over the road, was almost more than she could take. She says she had her hand on the key but couldn't bring herself to start the car up and drive straight ahead. There was a moment where she'd thought she could do it, drive over Henry and be done with it, but the moment passed.

"Why?" I asked her. "Why didn't you run when you saw him coming over the hill?"

144

"BECAUSE HE WAS REACHING OUT TO ME, LIKE BEFORE, AT ST. MARK'S. AND I REALIZED THEN THAT HE WASN'T TRYING TO REACH OUT AND GRAB ME. HE WAS TRYING TO REACH OUT AND GIVE ME SOMETHING. AND THERE WAS SOMETHING ELSE. HE WAS DYING."

I ASKED HER HOW SHE KNEW THIS AND SHE SAID I WOULD HAVE KNOWN, TOO. HE WAS MOVING SO SLOWLY, DRAGGING HIS DESTROYED LEG, WOBBLING DOWN THE HILL. IT WAS MENACING IN A GHOSTLY SORT OF WAY, BUT SHE KNEW, DEEP DOWN INSIDE, THAT IT WASN'T A GHOST AT ALL. IT WAS A MAN, A BROKEN MAN.

SHE SAID I'D NEED TO WATCH THE VIDEO FOR MYSELF TO SEE AND HEAR ALL THAT HAD HAPPENED. IT WAS JUST HER WAY TO SHOW ME, NOT TELL ME. IT WAS THE ONLY WAY SHE KNEW HOW TO SHARE THE REALLY BIG MOMENTS IN HER LIFE. I FELT A LITTLE SAD FOR HER THEN, BECAUSE I UNDERSTOOD WHAT SHE MEANT. I CAN NEVER TELL ANYONE HOW I REALLY FEEL. I ALWAYS HAVE TO WRITE IT DOWN.

AND SO I'LL WRITE DOWN HOW I FEEL RIGHT NOW, SINCE I WON'T BE ABLE TO TELL ANYONE TOMORROW OR THE DAY AFTER THAT OR EVER.

145

I'm sad, if you want to know the truth. Sad that Henry wandered the country all alone, sick and broken. I've always had a problem with that sort of thing, people being all alone in the world, no matter how bad they are. In my darkest moments I imagine myself old and all alone, staring at a TV screen, wishing it would all just come to an end. My heart breaks just thinking about it.

I'm also feeling a deep sense of relief. I now realize that sometimes you don't know how stressed out you are until after it's passed. After the bad person in your life is gone. After the bad test is over, after some giant badness moves off like a storm cloud. I didn't know how scared I was until an hour ago when my fear died right along with the ghost of Old Joe Bush.

He can't get me anymore.

And, more important, he can't get Sarah anymore.

He's gone. They both are. The ghost of Old Joe Bush and Henry don't have any power over me any longer.

That part of my life is now in the past.

It would have been nice if they hadn't been replaced by the Raven, but I'll take what progress I can get.

I heard the same new sound in Sarah's voice, too.

"I know where the hideout for B and C is," she said.

"You're driving and talking on the phone," I said, ever the safety tzar of our lives.

"It's a dirt road after midnight. The only thing I'm going to hit is a cow."

"I feel sorry for the cow."

I asked her how she knew where the hideout was.

"He showed me."

It appeared that in the end, Henry wanted the same thing we did: to follow the A-postle all the way to the end. And that's exactly what we're going to do.

"He hasn't been reaching out to grab me," she said. "He's been trying to give me a message. Wanna hear it?"

I DID, BUT THE THOUGHT OF SARAH TALKING ON
HER CELL PHONE AND READING A NOTE WHILE DRIVING
DOWN A DIRT ROAD WAS MORE THAN I COULD PUT
UP WITH.

"WHOA, COW!" SHE SCREAMED.

ALWAYS WITH THE JOKES, THIS GIRL.

SHE STOPPED THE CAR AT THE DESERTED TURN
LEADING BACK TO THE HIGHWAY AND READ FROM THE
NOTE SHE'D FOUND CLUTCHED BETWEEN HIS DEAD
FINGERS. IT'S SHORT, SO IT WASN'T VERY HARD TO
WRITE DOWN IN MY JOURNAL. IT WAS RANDOM, LIKE
HE'D WRITTEN A LINE, THEN WAITED A WEEK TO WRITE
THE NEXT — NOT SO MUCH A LETTER AS A STREAM OF
UNCONNECTED THOUGHTS.

HERE IT IS, AS SARAH READ IT TO ME:

IT'S TIME TO GO, ME AND OLD JOE.

B AND C IS BONNIE AND CLYDE.

INVOKE THE CLAUSE!

I'M SORRY FOR ALL HE'S DONE.

SORRIER THAN YOU KNOW.

JOE

I've thought about what these words mean, and here are my conclusions:

— First and foremost, Henry had lost or was losing his mind. The note starts out as if it's Henry writing about him and the ghost of Old Joe Bush, and ends with Joe saying Henry is sorry. It's not clear to me Henry knew who he was at the end. As we'd suspected, something about the trauma of all those years guarding the dredge and playing the part of a ghost had gotten lodged too deeply in his brain. The guilt of all his past sins exposed and the great fall that shattered his leg only served to deepen his madness. Old Joe Bush had his leg pulled through the gears, Henry shattered his own falling in the same dredge. My guess? He was bleeding inside, needed a doctor but wouldn't turn himself in, and found his body and mind had turned against him. I think, in the end, he was neither Henry nor the ghost of Old Joe Bush. He was both.

— I BELIEVE TO THIS DAY THAT HENRY WAS A LIAR AND A THIEF, BUT I DON'T BELIEVE HE EVER INTENDED TO KILL ANYONE. HE WAS RESPONSIBLE FOR THE DEATHS OF THE APOSTLE AND DR. WATTS, AND HE NEARLY GOT ME KILLED. BUT I HAVE PERSONAL EXPERIENCE WITH THIS GUY, AND I'M TELLING YOU, THEY WERE ALL ACCIDENTS. THE BIGGEST PROBLEM HENRY HAD WAS BEING SOLD OUT TO THE CROSSBONES, WHICH MADE HIM DO THINGS HE WASN'T WIRED TO DO. I THINK HE TRIED TO SCARE PEOPLE INTO DOING WHAT HE NEEDED THEM TO DO BECAUSE HE DIDN'T HAVE IT IN HIM TO KILL IN COLD BLOOD.

— I THINK HENRY WAS TRYING TO HELP US AS ATONEMENT FOR ALL HIS SINS. THAT'S WHY HE RAN, WHY HE WOULDN'T TURN HIMSELF IN. HE PROTECTED SARAH ON HER JOURNEY WEST, EVEN AS HE WAS INCHING CLOSER TO DEATH'S DOOR. HE GAVE ME THE RAVEN PUZZLE IN THE PORTLAND UNDERGROUND. AND NOW HE'D GIVEN US THE SOLUTION TO THE B AND C HIDEOUT: BONNIE AND CLYDE. THE FAMOUS BANK ROBBERS FROM THE 1930s. WE SHOULD HAVE BEEN SMART ENOUGH TO

FIGURE THAT OUT, BECAUSE BONNIE AND CLYDE'S HIDEOUT WAS IN JOPLIN, MISSOURI, PART OF THE SPOOKSVILLE TRIANGLE.

— AND FINALLY, HE ASKS US TO INVOKE "THE CLAUSE." THIS STATEMENT IS A MYSTERY, BUT I THINK THE VIAL OF LIQUID ON ITS WAY TO SKELETON CREEK IS GOING TO SHOW US WHAT IT MEANS. HE WANTS US TO INVOKE "THE CLAUSE," SO THAT'S WHAT WE'RE GOING TO DO. I HOPE IT DOESN'T SET OFF A CROSSBONES NUCLEAR BOMB OR SOMETHING.

MY LAST WORDS ON THIS: HENRY HAD TO BE IN A LOT OF PAIN. HE LIVED A LIE HIS WHOLE LIFE AND HE WAS WANDERING THE EARTH ALONE AT THE END. HE TRIED TO MAKE THINGS RIGHT. AND NOW HE'S GONE, SOON TO BE FORGOTTEN. ALL IN ALL, THE GUY PAID A HEAVY PRICE.

REST IN PEACE.

SUNDAY, JULY 17, 1:40 A.M.

WE AGREED THAT I WOULD USE AN ANONYMOUS EMAIL
ACCOUNT TO SEND IN AN ALERT WHILE SARAH
CHECKED INTO HER HOTEL AND KEPT A LOW PROFILE.
EVERYONE IN SKELETON CREEK HAD BEEN GIVEN
AN EMAIL ADDRESS TO USE IF THEY STUMBLED ONTO
ANYTHING THAT MIGHT LEAD TO FINDING HENRY, SO I
KNEW JUST WHERE TO SEND IT. TOOK ME ABOUT A
MINUTE TO CREATE A BOGUS GMAIL ACCOUNT AND
ANOTHER MINUTE OR TWO TO TYPE IN WHAT I WANTED
TO SAY.

There's a dead guy at the Spooksville Triangle in Missouri. Look
it up online. You can't miss him. He's lying in the middle of the
road. I think it's that crazy guy from Skeleton Creek people have
been talking about. Anonymous.

WITH ALL THE OTHER ACTION FLYING AROUND
SKELETON CREEK, I WAS SURE THIS NEWS WOULD MAKE
IT TO THE MAYOR'S OFFICE IN NO TIME FLAT. BY
MORNING, HE'D BE KNOCKING ON MY DOOR WITH NEWS
OF HENRY'S DEATH. IT WOULD BE BITTERSWEET FOR

152

MY DAD, BUT IT WOULD ALSO ALLOW HIM TO REST EASIER KNOWING AN UNSEEN THREAT AGAINST HIS FAMILY HAD DEPARTED THE PLANET.

SARAH IS GOING TO HEAD FOR THE HOTEL IN JOPLIN, MISSOURI, AND CRASH FOR THE NIGHT. SHE'LL SLEEP LATE AND BOOK THE ROOM FOR A SECOND NIGHT, USING HER OWN MONEY. SOMETIME DURING THAT TWO-DAY BREAK, SHE'LL GO TO BONNIE AND CLYDE'S HIDEOUT AND FIND WHAT THE APOSTLE LEFT BEHIND.

HER PARENTS ARE GOING TO HEAR ABOUT HENRY FOR SURE. HOPEFULLY, THAT WON'T PUT AN END TO HER STOPS RIGHT AS WE'RE COMING TO THE FINAL LEG OF OUR JOURNEY.

SUNDAY, JULY 17, 4:05 P.M.

As I'd suspected, it was the mayor who delivered the news. About an hour ago, he landed on our front porch, where my mom and dad were reading the paper. I was inside, napping on the couch, when my mom called me out to join them.

"They found Henry," said Mayor Blake. "He's gone."

My mom seemed the most shook up at first, sitting down and staring at the old painted boards on our porch. She'd always liked Henry, and never really could bring herself to fully believe all the bad things he'd done.

"Where?" my dad asked. He, too, was moved by the news. "Where" was the only word he could muster.

"It's the strangest thing," the mayor continued. "He was out in the middle of nowhere. Someplace called the Spooksville Triangle on the border of Kansas and Missouri. What he was doing out there, I have no idea."

"How'd he die?" I asked, curious about whether or not they'd be searching for foul play.

The mayor said they didn't know for sure, but that it appeared Henry had never gotten medical attention after the fall in the dredge. His leg was bleeding internally, and he'd suffered a severe concussion.

"It was really just a matter of time," he concluded.

I couldn't tell how my dad was taking the news. He's a quiet guy by nature, especially so when bad things happen.

I ventured an important question.

"Who knows about this?"

The mayor could not have given me a better answer.

"I was just coming to that. The investigation is ongoing, for reasons I don't fully understand. In any case, the authorities would like us to keep this quiet for a few days until they can make an announcement. It would seem Henry had a complicated life both here and back east."

He went on to tell us that we were only being told because of all the things about Henry that were connected to our family. The

AUTHORITIES FIGURED WE DESERVED TO KNOW THERE WAS NO LONGER A MADMAN ON THE LOOSE.

IF ONLY THEY KNEW ABOUT THE AX-WIELDING RAVEN LIVING IN THE WOODS OUTSIDE SKELETON CREEK. OR MAYBE THE RAVEN IS EXACTLY WHY THEY DON'T WANT TO GO PUBLIC WITH THE NEWS JUST YET. MAYBE THEY'RE TRYING TO FLUSH OUT THE REALLY BAD GUY, AND LETTING HIM THINK HENRY IS STILL ALIVE HAS SOME PURPOSE.

EITHER WAY, IT'S EXCEPTIONALLY GOOD NEWS. I WAS LYING ON THE COUCH ALL MORNING THINKING OF HOW WE WERE EVER GOING TO KEEP SARAH ON THE ROAD ONCE HER PARENTS FOUND OUT ABOUT HENRY BEING IN THE SAME PLACE SHE WAS. THEY'D FLIP OUT FOR SURE. THEY'D MAKE HER DRIVE STRAIGHT HOME, NO MORE MAKING DOCUMENTARIES ABOUT SPOOKY PLACES. SHE'D NEVER GET TO SAVANNAH OR MONTICELLO, AND THE APOSTLE'S FINAL MESSAGE MIGHT BE HIDDEN FOREVER.

AS I GOT UP TO GO TO MY ROOM AND CALL SARAH, I HEARD MAYOR BLAKE TALKING TO MY PARENTS ABOUT HENRY. HE WAS ALREADY SPINNING IT INTO HIS PR MACHINE.

"I'D LIKE TO SEE IF WE CAN GET HIM BURIED HERE IN TOWN, IF YOU ALL DON'T MIND."

A-NOTHER STOP IN THE EVOLVING SKELETON CREEK TOURIST TRAP.

YIPPEE.

Sunday, July 17, 4:24 p.m.

Just called Sarah, but she didn't pick up. I'm sure she's catching up on her sleep, but I can't help worrying about her. I left her a voice message about word of Henry's death reaching Skeleton Creek, but that it was an open investigation not to be discussed outside of my own family.

With any luck at all, Sarah will be back in Boston before the news breaks.

Nothing to do now but wait.

Wait for a vial of liquid to show up in the mail tomorrow.

Wait for Sarah to wake up.

Wait for another message from the Apostle.

I feel like I'm crawling out of my own skin.

SUNDAY, JULY 17, 10:10 P.M.

JUST WHAT THE DOCTOR ORDERED ON A SUNDAY
THAT SEEMED TO GO ON FOREVER! SARAH DID IT TO
ME AGAIN. SHE WENT TO THE BONNIE AND CLYDE
HIDEOUT BEFORE CHECKING INTO THE HOTEL LAST NIGHT
AND DIDN'T BOTHER TO TELL ME. AFTER THAT, SHE
SLEPT UNTIL NOON, THEN SPENT THE NEXT TEN HOURS
EDITING TOGETHER A BUNCH OF NEW STUFF FOR ME TO
LOOK AT. HOLED UP IN A HOTEL ROOM IN MISSOURI
WITH NO DISTRACTIONS GAVE HER A CHANCE TO
REALLY DIG IN AND CUT SOME NICE FOOTAGE.
HERE'S THE NOTE SHE SENT ME:

Wait until you see the video of the night the ghost of Old Joe Bush
came up over the hill. If I didn't know better, I'd say it really *was* a
ghost. Henry is dead, but I'm not ready to say the ghosts have been put
to rest.

I should have called you last night, but you sounded so out of it, I figured
why worry you? Instead of going to the hotel right away, I went ahead
and drove over to Bonnie and Clyde's hideout. Everything went fine —
it was actually the easiest find yet. No ghosts, no visitors — it was all
very routine. I found the stone marked A, right at the base of the house

in the back corner, and pried it off. In there? A burlap bag with a Crossbones birdie stamped on it. You'll have to watch the video to see what was in there and what I did with it. Crazy!

I'm giving you three videos this time — been editing nonstop! Ten hours of sleep makes me hyper-productive.

Call me after you've watched!

Password: spooksville

I can hardly wait to get on the road. Next stop, Savannah, Georgia.

Finally tired. 'Night!

Sarah

THESE ARE AMAZING VIDEOS — THE APOSTLE GETS CLOSE TO SPILLING THE BEANS ABOUT THE AUTHOR OF THE GHOST BOOK. WHICH BEGS THE QUESTION . . . CAN THERE BE AN AUTHOR OF A BOOK WITH NO WORDS? AND SEEING THE GHOST OF OLD JOE BUSH ONE LAST TIME IS KIND OF INCREDIBLE. I'M WITH SARAH: IF YOU ASK ME, THIS IS ONE GHOST THAT WILL NEVER GO COMPLETELY OUT OF EXISTENCE.

SARAHFINCHER.COM
Password:
SPOOKSVILLE

SUNDAY, JULY 17, 11:04 P.M.

I DON'T KNOW HOW SARAH KEEPS GOING. THE ROAD IS
A LONELY AND SCARY PLACE, BUT SOMEHOW, SHE
MANAGES TO MAKE IT LOOK LIKE SHE'S HAVING A
PRETTY GOOD TIME OUT THERE. I ADMIRE THAT. IF IT
WERE ME, I'D BE COMPLAINING ENDLESSLY.

A-NOTHER LETTER FROM THE A-POSTLE: P. SO
NOW WE'VE GOT AN A- AND A P — ONLY ONE LETTER
TO GO. I DON'T SEE HOW ONE MORE LETTER IS GOING TO
ADD UP TO ANYTHING, BUT HOPEFULLY THE A-POSTLE
WILL TELL US SOMETHING MORE WHEN WE SEE HIM
AGAIN. FOR NOW, WE'VE GOT THE RAVEN PUZZLE
FILLED IN WITH ANOTHER LETTER:

AND IN THE BURLAP SACK? ANOTHER VIAL OF
LIQUID, ONLY THIS TIME THERE'S NO LABEL ON IT.

SARAH JUST SENT ME ANOTHER EMAIL. I'LL LET
HER DESCRIBE WHAT WAS IN THE VIAL.

Ryan,

I couldn't wait to see what you thought — this vial's gross, right? Looks
like it's filled with black tar, and it has one of those wax seals on the
top. Also, it has a red ribbon on the neck that reminds me of blood (I
don't know why). There's something very gothic about this vial, Ryan.
Something, I don't know, sinister, I guess. I think it might be poison.

I set it in the bathroom. Couldn't stand looking at it anymore.

Sarah

I CAN SEE A STORY HERE: VIAL OF BLACK GOO
CRAWLS INTO UNSUSPECTING GIRL'S EAR, TURNS HER INTO
A ZOMBIE. THIS IS GETTING BAD. I HAVE TWO VIALS
FILLED WITH WHAT? POISON? SOME SORT OF
ALCHEMY CONCOCTION MADE BY DR. WATTS? THEY
COULD BE FILLED WITH A LOT OF DIFFERENT THINGS.

Times like these, I wish I were a chemist with a laboratory in my basement.

She's sending me the vial tomorrow so it will arrive on Tuesday. By then Sarah should be all the way over to Monticello. The toughest part of her journey will be over.

Somehow, I think the hardest part of mine will just be starting.

My mom just knocked on my door with a message from the mayor: I'm to appear at his office at 9:00 a.m. sharp for an in-depth interview with Albert Vern of the <u>Washington Post</u> . . .

. . . and Gladys Morgan is going to join me.

"He says the reporter is stopping in for the morning, then he's on some assignment with the president. Can you believe that?"

Wow, I guess Albert Vern is even more important than I thought.

"It's now or never," my mom said.

How about never?

"Not a word about Henry," my mom added. She grilled me about Sarah — wasn't she on some road trip home from summer film school? I said I thought so, but that we really hadn't talked much lately.

My mom didn't buy it, but neither did she seem overly concerned. If only she knew that Sarah had been standing over Henry when he kicked the bucket.

I GUESS THE INTERVIEW WON'T BE THAT BAD. I MEAN,
AT LEAST ALBERT VERN IS A FISHERMAN. WE STICK
TOGETHER. AND IT WILL KILL SOME TIME WHILE I
WAIT FOR THE MAIL TO SHOW UP SO I CAN SEE THIS
MYSTERIOUS VIAL FOR MYSELF AND GET IT INTO FITZ'S
HANDS.

SEEING MY MOM AND KNOWING ABOUT THIS
INTERVIEW MAKES ME NERVOUS. WHEN THE GUY
DELIVERS THE MAIL, HE USUALLY SHOWS UP BETWEEN
10:00 A.M. AND 11:00 A.M., WHICH MEANS HE'S
PROBABLY BUZZING AROUND TOWN DURING THAT HOUR
DELIVERING ALL THE MAIL-ORDER STUFF MY NEIGHBORS
BUY. I CAN'T HAVE MY MOM GETTING THAT PACKAGE.

INTERVIEW STARTS AT 9:00 A.M. I'LL MAKE IT
MY GOAL TO BOLT BY 10:00 A.M., JUST IN CASE.
THEN I'LL WAIT ON THE PORCH FOR MY PACKAGE.

Monday, July 18, 11:14 a.m.

I am not a swearing man, but if I was, I'd be cursing up a storm right now. Dang that Gladys Morgan and Mayor Blake! Neither one of them would let me leave until we answered each and every question Mr. Vern had. I could have done the entire thing in twenty minutes flat, but oh no, Gladys had to go all hyper-detail on me. I'd give a thirty-second, twenty-word answer, and she'd follow up with ten minutes of drivel. It was excruciating!

Here's a real zinger: The missing Jefferson library was under your nose all along. What does that mean to a town like Skeleton Creek?

My reply: We're very proud. It's awesome.

Gladys Morgan's reply: Add ten minutes of GRADE-A BORING to my perfectly crafted answer. Now, times that by twenty questions and you'll understand why I had to run home only to arrive on the front steps of my house at 11:04 a.m.

LUCKILY FOR ME, MOM WASN'T HOME, SO NOW I'M SITTING ON THOSE SAME STEPS WITH A GLASS VIAL OF SUPERSECRET LIQUID IN MY FRONT POCKET. THE DELIVERY GUY LEFT IT BY THE FRONT DOOR IN A SHOE BOX WRAPPED IN BROWN PAPER. INSIDE THE SHOE BOX, SARAH HAD WRAPPED THE VIAL IN THE EQUIVALENT OF A WEEKS' WORTH OF LOCAL NEWSPAPERS.

NOW ALL I HAVE TO DO IS GET THIS THING OUT TO FITZ'S OLD TRAILER BEFORE NOON, WHEN MY DAD EXPECTS ME TO SHOW UP AT THE SHOP AND WORK THE REST OF THE DAY. NO PROBLEM THERE — THE TRAILER IS ON A DIRT ROAD OUTSIDE OF TOWN — I CAN GET THERE AND BACK WITH TIME TO SPARE.

I TEXTED SARAH TO LET HER KNOW I GOT THE PACKAGE AND SHE FIRED ONE RIGHT BACK:

ON THE ROAD TO SAVANNAH. CAN HARDLY WAIT! ALWAYS WANTED TO GO THERE. PARENTS ARE GOOD. THEY'RE HAPPY I'M CLOSE TO HOME. I'LL LET YOU KNOW WHEN I SETTLE INTO ROOM 204. BOO!

LOVE THE BOO.

I HADN'T BEEN PAYING CLOSE ATTENTION TO HOW FAR AWAY SARAH WAS GETTING. IN A FEW HOURS, SHE'LL BE ABOUT AS DISTANT AS SHE CAN BE WITHOUT LEAVING THE UNITED STATES.

BUMMER.

GOT THE VIAL IN PLACE SO FITZ CAN FIND IT. I GLANCED THROUGH THE DUSTY WINDOWS THINKING MAYBE I COULD FIND A PICTURE OF THE RAVEN OR SOME OTHER CLUE. IT CROSSED MY MIND TO BREAK IN AND LOOK AROUND, BUT MAN, THAT PLACE GIVES ME THE CREEPS BIG-TIME. PLUS, IT WOULD BE A DISASTER IF I GOT CAUGHT OR QUESTIONED ABOUT A BREAK-IN AT THE OLD TRAILER. DRAWING ATTENTION TO MYSELF RIGHT ABOUT NOW FEELS LIKE A BAD IDEA.

I'M TEMPTED TO ASK MY DAD IF HE EVER CROSSED PATHS WITH FITZ'S DAD, BUT I KNOW WHAT THE ANSWER WILL BE. FITZ ALREADY TOLD ME HIS DAD WAS RECLUSIVE, AND WHEN HE SHOPPED HE ALWAYS WENT TO THE SAFEWAY IN BAKER CITY, DOWN THE ROAD.

"HE'S EITHER IN THE TRAILER, IN THE WOODS, OR DOING SOMETHING SECRET I DON'T KNOW ABOUT," FITZ ONCE TOLD ME. NO MATTER. EVEN IF HE DID COME INTO TOWN, HE WOULDN'T HAVE A BLACK HOOD ON, LOOKING LIKE AN EXECUTIONER. WHAT

GOOD'S IT GOING TO DO IF I KNOW WHAT HIS DAD

LOOKS LIKE?

By THE TIME I GET OFF WORK AT 6:00 P.M.,

SARAH SHOULD BE IN SAVANNAH, GEORGIA, DEALING

WITH THE GHOST OF A GIRL WHO DOVE INTO

PAVEMENT. OUCH.

MONDAY, JULY 18, 1:12 P.M.

ALBERT VERN JUST STOPPED INTO THE FLY SHOP TO
SAY GOOD-BYE AND ASK ME IF I WAS SURE THERE
WASN'T ANYTHING ELSE I'D LIKE TO SAY ON THE RECORD.
DAD LOOKED AT ME FROM ACROSS THE COUNTER AND I
THOUGHT FOR A SECOND HE WAS GOING TO SPILL THE
BEANS ABOUT HENRY. BUT HE STAYED QUIET AND SO
DID I. I'D SAID ALL I WAS GOING TO SAY ABOUT THE
DREDGE, THE GOLD, THE JEFFERSON LIBRARY —
ALL OF IT.

"WISH I HAD TIME TO HOOK A FEW MORE TROUT,"
VERN SAID WHEN HE REACHED THE DOOR. "KEEP
FINDING BURIED TREASURE AND MAYBE I'LL BE BACK."

AND THEN IT HAPPENED. I FREAKED OUT. I SLIPPED.
MY MIND WENT BLANK AND I JUST BLURTED IT OUT.

"YOU CAN COUNT ON IT. PROBABLY BY
TOMORROW."

ALBERT VERN WAS EYEING ME AS I SAID IT, AND
THERE WAS SOMETHING IN HIS EXPRESSION THAT MADE
ME NERVOUS. HE WAS A REPORTER AT THE TOP OF HIS
GAME AT ONE OF THE MOST PRESTIGIOUS PAPERS IN
THE WORLD. HE SMELLED SOMETHING MORE THAN A KID
BOASTING ABOUT WHAT HE THOUGHT HE COULD DO. IT

172

LOOKED AS IF HE'D CAUGHT THE THREAD OF A BIGGER STORY.

As the door closed behind Albert Vern, I WONDERED IF HE REALLY WAS LEAVING TOWN. MORE LIKELY, I'D JUST ALERTED A REPORTER WITH A SHOVEL TO START DIGGING FOR INFORMATION.

What could he get access to? Could he get INTO MY PHONE RECORDS IF HE WANTED TO? Could HE GET INTO Sarah's? What if he found all the VIDEOS? What if he figured out everything and BEAT Fitz to the vial?

A lot of what-ifs, all because I opened my big MOUTH.

Lesson learned, hopefully not too late.

MONDAY, JULY 18, 6:29 P.M.

SARAH SHOULD BE PULLING INTO SAVANNAH, GEORGIA, BEFORE DARK. SHE BETTER, OR HER PARENTS ARE GOING TO FLIP. I KNOW SHE SAYS THEY'RE NOT KEEPING CLOSE TABS ON HER, BUT SHE'S BEEN RIDING THE RAZOR'S EDGE OF THE RULES FOR DAYS. I'D HATE TO SEE HER PARENTS DRIVE DOWN THE COAST AND MEET HER SOMEWHERE. THAT WOULD COMPLICATE THINGS RIGHT AS WE'RE COMING TO THE END.

    P.S. YOU COULDN'T PAY ME ENOUGH MONEY TO STAY IN ROOM 204 AT THE 17 HUNDRED 90 BUILDING. IT'S TOTALLY HAUNTED.

SARAH ARRIVED IN SAVANNAH AND CHECKED INTO THE ROOM. IT DIDN'T TAKE HER ANY TIME AT ALL TO FIND WHAT SHE WAS LOOKING FOR AND SEND ME AN EMAIL.

Ryan,

I don't want to take chances calling you tonight. My parents are on high alert about this place. I guess my mom did some research on the hotel and she's losing her resolve when it comes to letting me run around ghost hunting.

I have to admit, there's something spooky about this room. No matter how many lights I turn on, it still seems dark in here. I looked out the window, saw the brick sidewalk below, felt movement in the room. Maybe I'm just really tired, but I would have bet my life someone was in the room with me.

But there was no one.

I found the air duct up in the corner, used a chair and a screwdriver.

Another Apostle video — maybe the last? Hopefully, it will give us the final letter and it will make some sense. I need to set up the projector and take a look, but I wanted to email you first so you know I got it. Plus, it makes me feel better to email you. Almost like you're here.

Keep your phone handy, will ya? This room is something else. I can't shake the feeling that someone is in here with me.

I might call if I get too freaked out.

Miss you. Exhausted.

Sarah

Oh, GREAT. Now I'm GOING TO HAVE TO STAY UP PRACTICALLY ALL NIGHT IN CASE SHE CALLS. WHO AM I KIDDING? I CAN'T STAY UP ALL NIGHT TO SAVE MY LIFE. I JUST TEXTED HER TO AT LEAST SEND ME THE LETTER THE APOSTLE LEFT IN HIS MESSAGE. I'M DYING TO KNOW WHAT IT IS.

<u>TEXT ME THE LETTER. IT WILL GIVE ME SOMETHING TO DO.</u> <u>HERE IF YOU NEED ME!</u>

A FEW MINUTES LATER:

<u>Working on that. Someone just jiggled the handle from the outside. When I opened the door, no one was there. Eek!</u>

Is she making that up or is someone actually following her? It's times like these I feel like running down the hall to my parents' room and confessing the whole crazy mess.

Why is it the closer we get to solving a big mystery the more dangerous things seem to feel? Every day feels like one day closer to the edge of an abyss that threatens to devour both of us. Staying clear of that edge feels harder and harder, like it's got some kind of gravitational pull and it's drawing us near.

I set up my camera to record overnight, just in case, while I wait for Sarah to message me back. Then I sat at my desk and looked at the Raven Puzzle and the three letters we'd use once Sarah got to Monticello: an A, a P, and whatever letter the A-postle gave us in room 204.

MESSAGE FROM SARAH:

Hold your horses, cowboy. It takes time to set up the old projector and feed the reel in. Give me five.

Five minutes, which probably meant ten, and I'd have the last letter of the puzzle. Not that having it would solve anything. I'd gone through the entire alphabet and it didn't matter what letter I used, the three letters didn't make a bit of sense. I waited, kept staring at the Raven puzzle, pondered.

Three letters that have something to do with Thomas Jefferson's old estate. The solution totally eludes me.

MESSAGE FROM SARAH:

E. That's the letter the A-postle showed. Have fun figuring it out. Looks to me like we're dealing with an A-PE. I'm going to start recording to video. So tired.

As I suspected, the third letter is only slightly helpful. I was hoping for something else, like a symbol or an entire word that would bring this whole thing together.

A—P—E. Ape.

Ape on Jefferson's house.

Ape on a building.

King Kong?

Oh, brother.

I feel like Charlie Brown. Total failure.

TUESDAY, JULY 19, 1:09 A.M.

I JUST HAD ONE OF THE SCARIEST MOMENTS OF MY
LIFE, AND I'VE HAD SOME HUGE SCARES, SO THAT'S
SAYING SOMETHING. THE MOMENT PROVIDED ME WITH
THE ANSWER I'VE BEEN LOOKING FOR, THOUGH, SO I
GUESS IT WAS WORTH IT. I MIGHT HAVE LOST A YEAR OF
MY LIFE DUE TO STRESS OVERLOAD, BUT AT LEAST I
KNOW WHAT THE A-PE MEANS.

HERE'S HOW IT WENT DOWN.

I FELL ASLEEP AT MY DESK (PREDICTABLE, I KNOW).
THEN I STARTED DREAMING, OR AT LEAST I THOUGHT I
DID. SOMETIMES I CAN'T TELL WHERE THE NIGHTMARES
END AND MY LIFE PICKS UP. I WAS DREAMING THAT A
RAVEN WAS TAP-TAP-TAPPING ON MY WINDOWSILL.

THE RAVEN. TAPPING WITH THE EDGE OF AN AX
BLADE, ABOUT TO BASH THE GLASS OUT AND CLIMB INSIDE
MY HOUSE.

THE SOUND KEPT COMING AS THE POEM UNWOUND
LIKE A CLOCK SPINNING BACKWARD IN MY BRAIN.

ONCE UPON A MIDNIGHT DREARY,
WHILE I PONDERED, WEAK AND WEARY

Tap tap tap. The Raven outside my window, cloaked in black, watching me sleep.

In my dream — or had I awoken? — I stood and backed up to the door, reaching for the handle.

And then the Raven spoke, first in a whisper, then loud enough for me to hear him through my window.

Ryan. Ryan! Ryan! It's me! Open the window!

After that I was fully awake, walking to the window, because it wasn't the Raven after all. It was Fitz, come to pay me a visit on his way back to the cave.

"You scared me so badly I feel like I should slap you," I said when I opened the window. "How'd you get up here?"

"It's easy," he replied. Fitz was dressed all in black with a hood over his head, so it was easy to see how I could have gotten him confused with someone else. "Climbed up on the porch rail and onto the eave."

I asked him if he'd gotten the vial, and he told me he had.

"I think it's for the clause," I said.

"I do, too."

So we agreed. He hadn't brought it with him, which he felt stupid for just then, so we couldn't know if spreading what was in the vial on the clause would reveal some hidden message or not. We both hoped it would.

"How are you doing up there? In the cave, I mean."

Fitz shrugged meaningfully, as if it hadn't been going very well and he wished he could get away. He looked off toward the street below, trying to hide the sadness in his eyes. But I could see.

"Dad's not all bad. He's confused, mostly, is what I think," Fitz said, his big shoulders leaning in on the windowsill like slabs of concrete. I'd forgotten what a big guy he was. "The Crossbones is killing him."

I hadn't ever thought of it that way before. I was simply afraid of an ax-wielding man in black who appeared to have it out for me. Henry, the

Apostle, even the Raven — maybe they were all prisoners of the Crossbones. Maybe the Crossbones made them do the things they did.

"I gotta get back before he wakes up," Fitz told me. "Long walk in the dark and all."

I wished I could go with him, but there was no way. I'd done that walk a thousand times, but rarely in the dark by myself. It would be lonely and scary.

"Sorry I can't go with you. I would if I could."

"I know you would."

Fitz smiled at me, and I thought to myself, well, at least the Crossbones won't carry on past Fitz's dad. Fitz is way too nice a guy to go that route.

A few seconds later, he was gone, promising to let me know if the vial was of any use or not.

I closed my window, locked it, lay down on the bed. Checking my phone, I saw that Sarah hadn't tried to contact me again. Maybe she, too, had conked out. She'd sounded tired in her messages, like she was on the verge of exhaustion. Hopefully, she can sleep without being bothered by whatever haunted things go on in that place.

And that's when it happened. It was while I was lying there on the bed, staring at the ceiling and wondering about my two closest friends. Both of them were out in the cold of the world alone right then. Sarah in a haunted hotel room, braving the night almost a thousand miles from home. Fitz walking a dark river path to a wooded clearing, and then to a cave darker still.

A--P-E, I whispered.

Tap. Tap. Tap.

A--P-E. Tap Tap Tap.

Not A--P-E. That's not right at all. It's not about a giant monkey. It's something darker, like the darkness of the cave in the deep wood.

E-A--P. That's the order of the letters. Tap tap tap goes the Raven on my windowsill.

And we all know who wrote the poem I'm getting at.

Edgar Allan Poe. E-A--P.

I GOT OUT OF BED AND WENT TO MY DESK AND STARTED WRITING THIS JOURNAL ENTRY, MY HAND SHAKING SO BADLY I HAD TO STOP AND TAKE THREE OR FOUR DEEP BREATHS. SOON, I HAD THE RAVEN PUZZLE BEFORE ME, AND THE WHOLE THING FELT SUDDENLY DRENCHED WITH MEANING. THE GOTHIC MADNESS OF EDGAR ALLAN POE WAS SMEARED ALL OVER IT.

I UNDERSTOOD. THERE WOULD BE NO NEED TO VISIT THOMAS JEFFERSON'S OLD HOME AT MONTICELLO. I'D FIGURED THAT OUT, TOO. THE DRAWING SAID TO PUT THE LETTERS IN THE MIDDLE, BUT IF YOU TOOK THE MIDDLE OUT OF THE HOUSE ON THE BACK OF A NICKEL, IT WASN'T A BUILDING AT ALL.

IT WAS A TOMBSTONE.

That part of the puzzle was meant as a clue, not as a place to visit where something might be found. No, where we would find what we were looking for is a hundred and sixty miles away in Baltimore, Maryland.

Edgar Allan Poe's tombstone.

It's where we're going to find the very end.

EMAIL FROM SARAH, SENT THREE HOURS AGO.

Ryan,

I got your note first thing this morning when I woke up. Chilling, to say the least. But good, too. Baltimore is one step closer to home, and it's only three hours from the hotel near Monticello where I'm staying. I'll wrap things up here. I didn't make the post yesterday, so I'll get the black vial in the overnight to you before I leave Savannah, then hit the road. (By the way, you SO owe me for postage. These packages are crushing my dining budget — Slurpee for lunch, here I come.)

New password for you with a documentary I made about room 204 and the Apostle footage: theredroom1849

A note on the documentary: After staying a night in room 204, I'm of the opinion that it is, in fact, haunted. You know me — I'm a debunker by nature — but I'm telling you, something is in that room, and it's not of this world. It's angry, sad, not at rest. Needless to say, I didn't sleep at all last night.

A note on the Apostle video before you watch it: It's the last one. We've reached the end of the journey.

If I have time, I'm going to work up a documentary on Edgar Allan Poe. He's more important to all this than I thought.

He's been here all along, hasn't he?

Sarah

THAT'S EXACTLY WHAT I WAS THINKING, THAT POE HAS BEEN HIDING IN THE SHADOWS FROM THE START. ALL THE WAY BACK TO THE VERY BEGINNING, WHEN I WAS LAID UP IN A HOSPITAL, MY LEG SHATTERED AND MY HEAD POUNDING — HE WAS THERE. HE'S ALWAYS BEEN THERE, HAUNTING MY DREAMS AND FILLING MY MIND WITH WILD IDEAS. IF EVERY WRITER HAS THE SPIRIT OF SOME PAST, DEAD WRITER LIVING INSIDE HIM, THEN EDGAR ALLAN POE ISN'T BURIED IN A CEMETERY IN BALTIMORE — HE'S BURIED IN THE DEEPEST, DARKEST PART OF MY SOUL, DIGGING HIS WAY OUT IN MY WORDS, TRYING TO FIND THE LIGHT OF DAY.

SARAHFINCHER.COM
Password:
THEREDROOM1849

TUESDAY, JULY 19, 7:02 P.M.

THE APOSTLE HAS VANISHED LIKE VAPOR IN THE AIR.
HE'S GONE, AND I REALIZE NOW THAT ONLY ONE
REMAINS: THE RAVEN. I HAVE A FEELING, DEEP DOWN IN
MY BONES, THAT THE CROSSBONES IS ALL BUT WIPED
OFF THE FACE OF THE EARTH. THEIR THREE-PART
MISSION FEELS LIKE SOMETHING SITTING AT THE BOTTOM
OF A BOX IN AN ATTIC, LEFT OVER FROM A TIME LONG
PAST WHERE SUCH THINGS HAD A PLACE IN THE WORLD:

1) PRESERVE FREEDOM.
2) MAINTAIN SECRECY.
3) DESTROY ALL ENEMIES.

ONLY ONE GUY LEFT LIVING BY THAT CODE, AND
HE'S GOT HIS SIGHTS SET ON ONE ENEMY.
ME.
TODAY, I HAVE WANTED THE COMFORT OF MY
JOURNAL AND NOTHING MORE. ALL DAY I WISHED FOR
A PEN AND PAPER, TO FEEL THE SECURITY OF WORDS
TRAPPED ON PAGES. I PUT THEM IN, THEY CAN'T GET
OUT. AND THE WORLD CAN'T GET IN. THESE WORDS
ARE A PRISON WITH BARS TO KEEP THE RAVEN AWAY.

190

I'M BEING FOLLOWED. I HAVE VERY LITTLE DOUBT ABOUT THIS FACT. IT'S A FEELING THAT PROBABLY ELUDES ANYONE WHO LIVES IN A BIG CITY. BUT OUT HERE, WHERE THERE ARE A THOUSAND TREES FOR EVERY PERSON, I CAN FEEL WHEN SOMEONE OR SOMETHING IS MOVING TOWARD ME. I DON'T HAVE TO SEE THEM. I COULD BE BLIND AS A BAT AND I'D KNOW.

I SPENT PART OF MY DAY RUNNING ERRANDS FOR MY DAD. TO THE POST OFFICE, OUT FOR LUNCH, TO THE GROCERY STORE FOR BOTTLES OF WATER AND CLIF BARS. EVERY TIME I LEFT THE SAFETY OF THE FLY SHOP I FELT IT, LIKE ICE ON MY NECK: THE RAVEN WATCHING ME.

SARAH WILL REACH MONTICELLO BY NIGHTFALL. SHE'LL CHECK INTO HER HOTEL — THE LAST HOTEL BEFORE RETURNING TO BOSTON — AND SHE'LL CALL HER PARENTS AND SAY SOMETHING LIKE, "YEAH, ALL TUCKED IN FOR THE NIGHT. CAN'T WAIT TO GET HOME TOMORROW. MISS YOU, TOO." THEN SHE'LL GET RIGHT BACK IN HER CAR AND DRIVE THREE HOURS UP TO BALTIMORE. THERE, SHE'LL EXAMINE EDGAR ALLAN POE'S GRAVE SITE. I CAN'T SAY THAT I'M THRILLED. FOR ONCE, I WISH IT WERE ME STANDING AT A

GRAVESTONE AFTER MIDNIGHT. I THINK STANDING AT POE'S GRAVE MIGHT BRING ME A SENSE OF RELIEF, OF HAVING COME FULL CIRCLE.

I KNOW TOO MUCH ABOUT THIS GUY. FOR EXAMPLE, I KNOW THAT THE GRAVESTONE SARAH IS GOING TO SEE IS NOT THE ONE THAT WAS ORIGINALLY PREPARED FOR MR. POE'S BURIAL PLOT. THAT ONE WAS MADE, BUT NEVER PUT TO USE. INSTEAD, IT WAS STRUCK BY A TRAIN RUN OFF ITS TRACKS, BROKEN INTO A THOUSAND PIECES. THIS KIND OF THING WAS ALWAYS HAPPENING TO EDGAR ALLAN POE: THINGS SNATCHED AWAY WITHOUT WARNING OR REASON. EVEN IN DEATH HE COULDN'T ESCAPE THE RANDOM CRUELTY OF LIFE.

AND SO HE WAS BURIED IN AN UNKNOWN PLOT, WITHOUT A HEADSTONE OR A MARKING. THIS FOR THE MAN WHO INVENTED MYSTERIES, SCIENCE FICTION, AND HORROR. LIKE VAN GOGH BEFORE HIM, POE WAS AN ARTIST REVERED IN DEATH, NOT THE LEAST BIT APPRECIATED IN LIFE.

SOMETIME LATER, A CHEAP SANDSTONE MARKER WAS PLACED OVER THE BURIAL PLOT WITH THE NUMBER 80, NOTHING MORE. AND LATER STILL, MONEY WAS RAISED IN ORDER TO BUILD A PROPER GRAVE SITE.

Unfortunately, even this effort ended in a final offense that remains to this day. Poe's birthday is engraved as the 20th of January, but he was born on the 19th. Insult piled on top of insult. After all he's given us, we can't even get the man's birthday right.

Maybe that's why I don't show anyone the stories I work on. I'd just as soon skip the part where nobody cares and I die in obscurity without having someone from some magazine say my stories lack depth or my character development is weak. No thanks.

Later on, long after I'm gone, someone will find my stories and be like — wow, I totally would have read this guy when he was alive, what a shame. But I know the truth. Nobody would have cared. Critics would have ripped me apart. They'd have been cruel.

I love to write, especially when I'm feeling miserable and paranoid.

This was fun.

WEDNESDAY, JULY 20, 12:06 A.M.

THE CALL CAME IN, ONE MINUTE PAST MIDNIGHT, SARAH STANDING BEFORE THE POE GRAVE. IT SITS INSIDE A CHURCH GATE, OFF IN THE GRASS, AWAY FROM THE MONUMENT. THE HEADSTONE IS SUPPOSED TO DENOTE THE LOCATION WHERE POE WAS ACTUALLY BURIED, WHICH IS SEPARATE FROM THE MONUMENT ERECTED CLOSER TO THE STREET.

"THERE'S A RAVEN ON THE TOP," SHE WHISPERED, BECAUSE IT WAS AFTER HOURS AND SHE'D CLIMBED OVER THE STONE RAIL INTO THE CEMETERY. "AND THE WORDS 'QUOTH THE RAVEN, NEVERMORE.'"

I HAD TO TELL HER IT WAS THE LAST LINE OF THE EIGHTH STANZA IN HIS MOST FAMOUS POEM, A HEARTBREAKING EPITAPH.

BUT THAT'S NOT THE INFORMATION SHE WAS THERE TO GET. THE RAVEN PUZZLE HAD MADE IT CLEAR: LOOK ON THE BACK RIGHT CORNER, DOWN BY THE GRASS.

"I DIDN'T SEE ANYTHING AT FIRST, BUT THEN I DUG A LITTLE INTO THE GRASS RIGHT AT THE BASE OF THE HEADSTONE," SHE SAID. I WAS, AS USUAL, AMAZED. WHO DIGS AROUND THE EDGE OF EDGAR ALLAN POE'S GRAVE IN THE DARKEST PART OF THE NIGHT?

194

"I DON'T THINK YOU'RE GOING TO LIKE WHAT IT SAYS."

I HAD ALREADY BEEN WONDERING ABOUT THIS. IN MY HEART OF HEARTS, I'D ALWAYS KNOWN. I KNEW IT BEFORE SHE SAID IT, KNEW IT FROM THE START.

ALL ROADS LEAD TO SKELETON CREEK.

"ARE YOU READY?" SHE ASKED ME.

"NOPE."

"TOO BAD."

AND THEN SHE TOLD ME WHAT SHE'D FOUND. SHE COULDN'T SAY WHETHER IT WAS PART OF THE ORIGINAL CARVING IN THE STONE OR IF SOMEONE HAD CARVED IT AFTER. BUT THERE IT WAS, FILLED IN WITH MUD, WHICH ACTUALLY MADE IT EASIER TO READ WITH A FLASHLIGHT.

"SC: PLOT 42"

WE BOTH KNEW WHAT IT MEANT. FOR SOME REASON, WHEN SHE SAID IT, I LAUGHED. IT ALL FELT SO RIGHT, LIKE EVERY PART OF OUR EFFORT HAD LED TO THE ONLY PLACE IT COULD LEAD IN THE END. SC: SKELETON CREEK. PLOT 42: THE OLD CEMETERY ON THE HILL. THERE WERE TWO CEMETERIES IN SKELETON CREEK, THE NEWER ONE AT THE FAR END

OF TOWN, AND THE OLD ONE ON THE HILL. NO ONE HAD BEEN BURIED IN THE OLD ONE FOR A WHILE, LIKE A HUNDRED YEARS, AND IT WAS IN POOR CONDITION. ALL THOSE HEADSTONES WERE NUMBERED, THAT MUCH I KNEW. IT WAS THE WAY THINGS WERE DONE IN A SMALL TOWN LONG AGO, JUST LIKE THE NUMBER 80 ON EDGAR ALLAN POE'S GRAVESTONE.

AND HOW ABOUT THAT NUMBER, 42? EVERYTHING ALL COMING TOGETHER LIKE A PUZZLE NOW, THE SAME NUMBER AS THE DREDGE.

WHATEVER FINAL SECRET THE CROSSBONES WAS HIDING, IT WOULD BE BURIED UNDER HEADSTONE NUMBER 42. I'D NEED A SHOVEL AND A LOAD OF COURAGE. THE SHOVEL I COULD GET EASY ENOUGH. THE COURAGE WAS ANOTHER MATTER ENTIRELY.

"YOU CAN DO THIS, RYAN." SARAH COULD SENSE MY DEEP HESITATION IN THE SILENCE THAT HUNG ON THE LINE. "AND YOU HAVE TO DO IT NOW, NOT TOMORROW OR THE NEXT DAY. RIGHT NOW. WAITING ISN'T GOING TO MAKE IT ANY EASIER. AND MORE IMPORTANT, WAITING IS GOING TO MEAN SOMEONE ELSE COULD FIND IT FIRST."

She was right, of course. For all I knew, Albert Vern had already tapped into my phone or figured out a way to put a tail on Sarah from back at the Washington Post. What would happen if he figured this whole thing out and beat us to the location? I could already read the headline in the paper: Reporter Uncovers Deepest Mystery Yet in Skeleton Creek, Outdoes Local Hero.

I can live with that. The problem? Sarah can't. After all she's done, she'll never forgive me if I don't get my sorry self out of this room and up on that hill before dawn.

"Remember what we talked about before," she said. "How you gotta get out there or life will pass you by? Those journals aren't going to give you a life. You have to go out and take it."

I think she's wrong about that. Minus Sarah, I think writing is the best part of my life. It makes me happy. So sue me.

"I'm going back to my hotel now," she said. "And tomorrow I'll be going home. The end is up

TO YOU, AND I'M GLAD FOR THAT. I TELL YOU WHAT —
DIG THE GRAVE AND I'LL COME OUT AND SEE YOU.
How's THAT FOR INCENTIVE?"

IT <u>WAS</u> A STRONG INCENTIVE. AND I FIGURED SHE
COULD DO IT. SHE'D TALKED HER PARENTS INTO
LETTING HER DRIVE ACROSS THE COUNTRY ONCE, WHY
COULDN'T SHE DO IT AGAIN? OR BETTER YET, MAKE IT
EASIER AND TAKE A DANG AIRPLANE THIS TIME.

"CALL ME WHEN YOU LAND," I SAID, THINKING OF AN
AIRPLANE BUT MEANING WHEN SHE LANDED IN HER
HOTEL. "I'LL GET IT DONE."

I SAT IN MY ROOM FOR TEN MINUTES.

THEN I THOUGHT ABOUT HOW MUCH SARAH WOULD
WANT TO SEE WHAT I WAS DOING, SO I TOOK A ROLL OF
SILVER DUCT TAPE OUT OF MY DESK DRAWER. A GUY
CAN MAKE JUST ABOUT ANYTHING OUT OF DUCT TAPE.
I FASHIONED A LITTLE POCKET FOR MY PHONE AND
HELD IT AGAINST ONE OF MY BASEBALL CAPS. THEN I
WRAPPED DUCT TAPE AROUND THE POCKET AND THE
HAT AND PUT IT ON. NOW I COULD RUN MY PHONE'S
VIDEO CAMERA AND DIG UP A GRAVE AT THE SAME
TIME. IT WAS A VERY SARAH THING TO DO.

I PULLED OUT THE GHOST BOOK AND WISHED I KNEW WHAT IT MEANT, WISHED FITZ HAD NEVER GIVEN IT TO ME IN THE FIRST PLACE. I TOOK OUT MY COLLECTION OF POE STORIES AND TURNED TO THE END OF "THE PIT AND THE PENDULUM." I'D READ IT TEN OR TWELVE TIMES AND FELT ITS POWER.

HE SPOKE TO ME THEN, DOWN THROUGH TIME, ONE WRITER TO ANOTHER. AND I FELT AS HE MUST HAVE FELT ALL THE DAYS OF HIS LIFE.

THERE WAS A LOUD BLAST AS OF MANY TRUMPETS! THERE WAS A HARSH GRATING AS OF A THOUSAND THUNDERS! THE FIERY WALLS RUSHED BACK! AN OUTSTRETCHED ARM CAUGHT MY OWN AS I FELL, FAINTING, INTO THE ABYSS.

I FEEL THAT WAY NOW, AS IF I'M FALLING INTO AN UNMARKED GRAVE, ALREADY FORGOTTEN BY ANYONE WHO EVER LOVED ME AND EVERYONE WHO NEVER KNEW ME. I AM FALLING, FALLING, FALLING INTO THE ABYSS.

I WON'T RETURN UNTIL I DIG UP THE GRAVE MARKED 42.

WEDNESDAY, JULY 20, 3:19 A.M.

I'M NOT DEAD.

SARAHFINCHER.COM
Password:
THECLAUSE

Wednesday, July 20, 3:39 a.m.

Sarah knows everything now. She's safe, which makes me happy. Pretty soon she'll be sleeping, and after that she'll wake up and drive home. I'll be happier still when I know she's off the road for good.

She immediately took what I shot at the cemetery and put it up at her site. I wanted her to see it first, to know what I know before I write it down.

She said I sounded like I was in shock. She said I didn't sound like myself. I haven't slept in a long time and everything about what happened after my long walk to the old cemetery is a brain melter. I'm still putting it all together.

Every story, fact or fiction, has its own way of unfolding. There is purpose to the way we craft these things. So Sarah has the images, but I'm still going to write what happened.

MY LEG BEGAN TO FAIL ME AND I STARTED TO LIMP AS I WALKED DOWN THE STREET WITH THAT SHOVEL IN MY HANDS. I'D PUT THAT LEG THROUGH A LOT DURING THE PAST FEW DAYS — RIDING DOWN TO SEE FITZ, CROSSING THE RIVER, MOVING THROUGH THE WOODS — AND IT WAS FINALLY SAYING, <u>HEY, DUDE, ENOUGH ALREADY.</u>

A DOG WHINED OFF IN THE DISTANCE AND I IMAGINED IT WAS HIT BY A CAR, WOBBLING OFF INTO A DITCH TO DIE. OTHER THAN THAT, IT WAS A STILL NIGHT IN SKELETON CREEK AS I APPROACHED THE HILLTOP GRAVEYARD. I LOOKED BACK OVER MY TOWN AND HEARD THE DOG ONCE MORE. IT WASN'T LIKE STARING OUT OVER A CITY AT NIGHT WITH ITS SEA OF LIGHTS. SKELETON CREEK, FROM UP HERE, LOOKED AS SECRET AND HAUNTED AS IT ALWAYS HAD. A PORCH LIGHT HERE AND THERE, A DARKENED MAIN STREET, THE SHADOWY OUTLINES OF TREES AND HOUSES.

I SEARCHED THE GRAVEYARD IN SILENCE AS A SOFT WIND DRIFTED OVER THE HILLTOP. WITH A FLASHLIGHT IN ONE HAND AND A SHOVEL IN THE OTHER, I CREPT CLOSE TO EACH STONE AND FOUND THEY HAD NO ORDER. I WOULDN'T FIND HEADSTONE 42 NEXT TO 41

NEXT TO 40. WHOEVER HAD ENVISIONED THIS PLOT OF LAND HADN'T BEEN IN POSSESSION OF AN ORDERED MIND. MORE LIKELY THEY'D DUG A HOLE IN WHATEVER OPEN SPACE THEY COULD FIND, DROPPED THE COFFIN INSIDE, AND PLANTED THE HEADSTONE. MAYBE THAT WAS THE WAY THINGS WERE DONE A HUNDRED YEARS AGO, OR MAYBE THE PERSON IN CHARGE JUST DIDN'T CARE. EITHER WAY, I SEARCHED FOR A WHILE BEFORE I CAME TO NUMBER 42.

THE NUMBERS WERE ON THE BACKS OF THE HEADSTONES, AND COMING AROUND THE FRONT, I HAD AN UNFORESEEN MOMENT OF TERROR. BECAUSE THERE IT WAS, THE NAME I SAW ON HEADSTONE NUMBER 42:

ALBERT VERN.

I STARED AT THE WORDS, AND, LIKE MAGIC, THE LETTERS BEGAN TO MOVE IN MY MIND. WHO WAS ALBERT VERN, IF NOT THE MAN HE'D CLAIMED TO BE?

THE FIRST LETTER REMAINED, HOT AND GLOWING IN MY BRAIN.

A

ALL THE REST OF THE LETTERS IN HIS FIRST NAME FELL AWAY, LIKE WHITE BONES OVER A CLIFF, TUMBLING INTO A BLACK SEA.

THE LAST NAME REMAINED: VERN.

AND THEN THE LETTERS STARTED TO MOVE, REARRANGING THEMSELVES AS I WISHED THEY WOULDN'T AND MY GRIP ON THE SHOVEL GREW TIGHTER.

THE MAN HAD NEVER BEEN A. VERN.

HE HAD ONLY EVER BEEN THE RAVEN.

THERE WAS A BRIEF MOMENT WHERE I STARTED TO SCREAM, OR TRIED TO, AT LEAST. MY THROAT HAD GONE DRY AND NOTHING BUT A WHIMPER CAME OUT. TOO BAD, MR. MAYOR. THERE IS NO REPORTER FROM THE WASHINGTON POST. ONLY A MAN WITH A BLACK AX SEARCHING FOR ANSWERS.

I KNEW THEN THAT ALBERT VERN HAD BEEN FOLLOWING ME ALL DAY. HE'D BEEN FOLLOWING ME ALL WEEK. HE KNEW I HAD THE GHOST BOOK. HE KNEW WHO'D GIVEN IT TO ME. AND WHAT WAS WORSE, HE'D ARRIVED IN THE CEMETERY, BLACK AS NIGHT, DRIFTING IN THROUGH THE TREES.

THE RAVEN APPROACHED WITH THAT SAME INHUMAN MOTION I'D SEEN BEFORE. THE GHOST OF OLD JOE BUSH MOVED LIKE THAT. FAR AWAY, THEN SOMEHOW STANDING RIGHT BESIDE ME.

And then he spoke.

"I've been following you."

He held the great ax in his hands, spun the blade, examined me carefully. Would I run away? Would I scream someone awake in the dead of night? He need not have worried: I was still like one of the tombstones, turned to stone with fear.

"I know what you stole from me."

I held the shovel as if it might protect me from the swinging ax.

"I know the Apostle led you here.

"I know what lies beneath the grave."

The Raven moved harrowingly close then, his face almost knowable, but still bathed in shadow. I wanted to point my flashlight in his eyes, but my mind and my hand wouldn't cooperate with each other.

"Step aside, son. Or meet your maker."

The Raven raised the ax over his head. If ever I needed to move, now was the time.

But I couldn't. Or at least, I didn't.

The ax hovered over the Raven's head, as if he was searching for a reason not to swing. And then a new voice boomed into the graveyard.

"I INVOKE THE CLAUSE!"

The Raven turned in the direction of the voice and light flashed over his face. The Raven, Albert Vern, Fitz's dad — these faces were one in the shadows and the gloom.

I couldn't take my eyes off his face. Was it an hour, a minute, a second that I stared into those eyes? Time had no meaning until I finally did turn to see what the Raven saw: Fitz, shadowy and big, holding the clause in one hand and a flashlight in the other. There were words on what was once an empty sheet of yellowed paper, brought back by whatever had been in the vial I'd given him.

With a voice of authority I hadn't heard before, Fitz read the clause.

"We believe in the everlasting supremacy of one generation after another.

We believe that the world is ever changing."

THE GREAT AX LAY AT THE RAVEN'S SIDE, AND HE BEGAN READING ALONG WITH FITZ, THEIR VOICES DRIFTING TOGETHER OVER THE STONES OF THE DEAD:

"WE GIVE POWER TO THE FIRSTBORN SON OF THE LAST MAN STANDING.

WE TRUST IN THE PASSING OF TIME AND THE KNOWING OF ALL THINGS.

THE DUTY TO PRESERVE FALLS NOW IN THE LINE OF ALL GOOD MEN."

THEY WERE BEAUTIFUL WORDS, STRONG AND MEANINGFUL. THEY HAD AUTHORITY. THE RAVEN FELL SILENT, AS IF HE'D WAITED HIS WHOLE ADULT LIFE TO HEAR THOSE WORDS, WONDERING WHEN THEY MIGHT BE SAID, KNOWING THEY WOULD HAVE POWER OVER HIM IN THE END. I WONDERED IF HE'D SAID THE WORDS HIMSELF A LONG TIME AGO, WRENCHING POWER FROM A LONG LINE OF MEN.

FITZ READ THE LAST OF THE CLAUSE ALONE WITHOUT EVEN LOOKING AT THE WORDS HE WAS SAYING.

"I TAKE THIS OATH

TO PRESERVE FREEDOM.

To maintain secrecy.

To destroy all enemies.

I appoint these three:

To protect: Sam Fitzsimons
To record: Sarah Fincher
To treasure: Ryan McCray
We are the Crossbones now."

Fitz paused and I looked back and forth
between the two. And then the son spoke the
last of the oath to his father, and there was a
sadness in those words I didn't see coming.

"Your time has passed."

The Raven never did take the hood off of his
head, but he did drop the ax. He left it lying
there in the cemetery and Fitz picked it up. I
had a strange sensation, seeing my friend there
with a weapon of some size. Was Fitz to be the
new muscle of the Crossbones? And more

IMPORTANT, WAS I TO BE ITS HENRY, AND SARAH ITS APOSTLE? THE VERY THOUGHT OF THESE THINGS LEFT ME FOGGY IN THE HEAD, AFRAID OF WHAT WAS TO COME IN THE MONTHS AND YEARS THAT WOULD FOLLOW.

WE BOTH WATCHED AS THE RAVEN — OR WHAT ONCE WAS THE RAVEN — DISAPPEARED INTO THE TREES. AFTER AN AWKWARD PAUSE, FITZ SPOKE.

"DID THAT JUST HAPPEN LIKE I THINK IT DID?"

I DIDN'T THINK ABOUT MY REPLY. I SIMPLY SAID IT, WHICH MADE IT FEEL TRUE EVEN IF IT WASN'T.

"I THINK WE'VE BECOME WHAT WE WERE FIGHTING ALL ALONG."

I LOOKED AT THE TOP OF THE GRAVE SITE AND I KNEW WHAT I SHOULD HAVE SAID.

STAND BACK. I'VE GOT SOME DIGGING TO DO.

BUT I DIDN'T, AND I CAN'T SAY EXACTLY WHY.

FITZ DIDN'T KNOW THERE WAS SOMETHING TO FIND AT GRAVESTONE NUMBER 42. HOW COULD HE? THE GUY HAD BEEN COOPED UP IN A CAVE FOR A WEEK. HE DIDN'T ASK FOR THE GHOST BOOK, WHICH SEEMED TO HAVE SLIPPED HIS MIND JUST THEN. HE simply said it was over, we'd ended the Crossbones.

"I think he wanted it to be over," Fitz told me, holding the ax in one big hand like a man of the woods. "Give him a few days chopping trees and I bet we'll be back at the trailer. It'll be like old times. I might even get my old job back at the fly shop."

I nodded, smiled weakly, let the words hang in the air. All I could think about was what lay under the ground I stood on.

"I need to go home," I said. "It's late."

"Yeah. I should probably follow my dad, make sure everything's okay."

Fitz said something about the clause and shook his head, hardly believing what had happened. But I felt it — we both did. Fitz's dad knew about the clause. He knew its power over the Crossbones, knew his time really had come and gone. The clause had achieved its cruel duty.

I walked maybe five minutes toward town as Fitz went the other way, then I stopped and

TURNED BACK. I WASN'T SCARED THIS TIME AS I STOOD
OVER THE GRAVE. I WAS EXCITED.

As I STARTED TO DIG I REALIZED WHAT I WAS DOING,
WHAT I'D BEEN DOING MY WHOLE LIFE.

I WAS KEEPING A SECRET.

It took about five minutes to find what I was digging for: a metal box a foot belowground that clanged when my shovel hit. There was a lock — not a very good one — but it didn't matter. It was a cheap sort of metal with crummy hinges that popped free with one blow from the shovel.

Inside was another wooden box, shaped like a coffin, only much smaller. It fit in my hand. When I opened the coffin and pointed my flashlight inside, there was a vial like the one I'd already given Fitz. Like the one Sarah was supposed to mail me right after she got it, but missed the deadline for overnight by an hour.

The black vial Sarah finally did mail that would arrive in Skeleton Creek in a few hours.

But this vial was different. Inside, white liquid, thick like Elmer's glue, and on the vial a short poem.

One part black, three parts white.
Make the Crossbones fear the night.

213

I PUT THE METAL BOX AND THE SMALL WOODEN COFFIN BACK IN THE GROUND AND BURIED THEM. THEN I MADE MY WAY HOME WITH THE VIAL IN MY POCKET, QUIETLY SNEAKING UP THE CREAKING STAIRS.

AND NOW I'M SITTING HERE, WIDE AWAKE WHEN I SHOULD BE SLEEPING. I'M WAITING FOR THE BLACK VIAL TO ARRIVE, SO I CAN MIX IT.

ONE PART BLACK, THREE PARTS WHITE.

AND THEN I'LL USE A BRUSH AND I'LL PAINT THE PAGES OF THE GHOST BOOK. AND IN THE GHOST BOOK I KNOW WHAT I'LL FIND.

SOMETHING SCARY.

Just got off the phone with Sarah. She's on her way home. I told her everything. At first she laughed — yeah right, you and me, Crossbones, that's a good one — but then she fell silent. Like me, I think she's wondering what that means, if anything.

I couldn't keep the white vial a secret from her. I even told her I'd kept it from Fitz.

"Good," she said. "I've never even met him. Let's wait and see what the ghost book tells us. No sense spilling the beans to the Raven's son just yet. Could be a trick."

I hadn't thought of that, but it didn't really add up. Fitz was a good guy, a friend. All he wanted was a normal life and a normal family. I could hardly begrudge him things like that.

"I guess this is the end, huh?" I said as we were wrapping things up.

"Either that," Sarah ventured, "or the very beginning. I mean, hey, we run the show now, right? Could mean a lot of things."

I couldn't help thinking it meant the three of us would be at war with one another one day.

I'm starting to wonder if I have trust issues.

Sarah left off by saying she'd been getting more and more interested in Edgar Allan Poe. The fact that this entire thing led to his tombstone really got her wheels spinning. So, in typical Sarah fashion, she's working on an Edgar Allan Poe documentary.

This girl acts more like the Apostle every day.

WEDNESDAY, JULY 20, NOON

Mom's working, dad's at the shop, I just ran out to grab us some lunch and stopped at the house. There was a small package at the door, as I'd hoped.

I have the black vial.

WEDNESDAY, JULY 20, 6:45 P.M.

SUSPENSE IS KILLING ME! I WON'T BE ABLE TO SNEAK
OFF TO MY ROOM UNTIL LATER TONIGHT, PROBABLY
NOT UNTIL THE SUN GOES DOWN. I WOULD HAVE
PREFERRED TO OPEN THE GHOST BOOK WHEN THE
SUN WAS STILL UP, BUT THAT'S NOT TO BE.

THE NEWS BROKE ABOUT HENRY. SOMEONE
BLABBED, OR MAYBE IT WAS SIMPLY TIME FOR THE
NEWS TO GET OUT. EVEN IN A TOWN KNOWN FOR
KEEPING SECRETS, HENRY'S DEATH WAS A HARD ONE
TO KEEP. SARAH IS BACK IN BOSTON, SAFE AND SOUND,
SO EVEN IF THEY DO QUESTION HER ABOUT WHERE SHE
WAS ON THE NIGHT THE BODY WAS FOUND, IT WON'T
MATTER THAT MUCH. SHE'S VERY GOOD AT COVERING
HER TRACKS. AND SHE'S OUT OF DANGER, SO I DON'T
THINK ANYONE IS GOING TO DIG TOO DEEPLY INTO IT.
HENRY WAS SICK AND DYING. HIS BODY HAD SIMPLY
LOST ITS ABILITY TO CARRY A SOUL AROUND. IT
HAPPENS. ESPECIALLY WHEN YOU'RE WALKING ALL
OVER KINGDOM COME, BLEEDING ON THE INSIDE.

IN ANY CASE, THE TOWN IS BUZZING TONIGHT. THE
MAYOR HAS HIS UNDERWEAR IN A BUNCH, AND ALL OUR
NEIGHBORS KEEP STOPPING BY TO SEE WHAT WE THINK.

Even Gladys Morgan, who doesn't get out much, sat on our porch and spent an hour trying to convince my dad to run for office. She kept saying Skeleton Creek was turning into a theme park and it had to stop and Paul McCray was just the guy to do it. My dad kept shaking his head, and my mom couldn't stop laughing. The idea of her quiet, unassuming husband running anything other than a fly shop, let alone an entire town, made it impossible to keep a straight face.

Time passes on the porch in Skeleton Creek. It's not as interesting as it sounds.

WEDNESDAY, JULY 20, 9:57 P.M.

Now that it's after dark, I have a mind to wait until midnight. Things seem more meaningful when one day is turning into the next.

So I'm waiting.

WEDNESDAY, JULY 20, 10:43 P.M.

I COULDN'T DO IT. FOUR MINUTES WAS ALL I COULD STAND BEFORE I HAD THE GHOST BOOK OPEN TO THE FIRST PAGE. I HAD A CEREAL BOWL FROM THE KITCHEN AND AN OLD WATERCOLOR PAINTBRUSH AND THE TWO VIALS.

AT FIRST, THINGS WENT VERY BADLY.

I DID LIKE I WAS INSTRUCTED: ONE PART BLACK, THREE PARTS WHITE. IT MADE A THICK, PASTY GRAY GOOP, AND WHEN I TESTED IT ON THE CORNER OF THE FIRST PAGE, THE PAGE BEGAN TO SIZZLE. THE WHOLE CORNER OF THE PAGE WAS EATEN AWAY BEFORE MY EYES.

WHATEVER SORT OF ALCHEMY OR CHEMISTRY WAS GOING ON HERE, THE TWO SUBSTANCES MIXED TOGETHER WERE WAY TOO POTENT FOR PAPER.

I SAT THERE FOR A FEW MINUTES ALL BUMMED OUT. MY FIRST SECRET AS A CROSSBONES MEMBER WAS A TOTAL DUD. IT WAS THE WATERCOLOR BRUSH THAT GOT ME THINKING.

WATERCOLOR.

THAT KIND OF PAINT STARTS OUT THICK. ADD WATER AND YOU GET THE RESULT YOU'RE LOOKING FOR.

221

I GOT A CUP OF WATER AND POURED IT INTO THE CEREAL BOWL, MIXING THE GRAY GOOP INTO A BUBBLY BROTH.

"CORNER NUMBER TWO," I SAID, FEELING LIKE I WAS TALKING TO THE BOOK. "TRY NOT TO BURST INTO FLAMES."

IT DIDN'T IGNITE OR SIZZLE LIKE BACON IN A FRYING PAN. INSTEAD, THE PAGE CHANGED COLOR. IT TURNED A SMOKY BROWN, LIKE IT WAS A PANCAKE THAT HAD JUST BEEN PERFECTLY COOKED.

I FILLED THE BRUSH AGAIN, AND THIS TIME, I RISKED PAINTING THE WATERY CROSSBONES BREW OVER THE FIRST PAGE OF THE BOOK.

MY BREATH CAUGHT IN MY THROAT AS THE ENTIRE PAGE TURNED TOASTY BROWN. BUT IT WASN'T ALL COLORED. SOME OF IT REMAINED AS IT WAS: PAPER YELLOWED WITH AGE.

WORDS. AND NOT JUST ANY WORDS. WORDS WRITTEN BY THE MASTER HIMSELF.

"NO WAY," I WHISPERED.

I'D SEEN HIS HANDWRITING BEFORE. AND BESIDES, HIS NAME WAS PLAIN AS DAY.

E. Poe — January the 4th, 1849

They're after me now. What an indignity!

I might have thought twice before bringing them into my confidence.

A mistake, no doubt. But this! Thrown to the dogs, left to rot.

It anguishes me, this deceit.

And so I shall make them pay all the days of their sorry lives.

THERE ARE NO WORDS TO DESCRIBE THE WAY I FELT WHEN I BEGAN READING THOSE WORDS. DON'T GET ME WRONG — MILLIONS IN GOLD AND A LIBRARY OF LOST BOOKS ARE NOT BENEATH MY INTEREST. BUT THIS WAS SOMETHING ALTOGETHER DIFFERENT.

THESE WERE WORDS NO ONE HAD EVER SEEN BEFORE.

THIS BOOK — THIS GHOSTLY BOOK ON EMPTY PAPER — IT WAS FILLED WITH EDGAR ALLAN POE'S WORDS. WORDS HIDDEN FROM THE WORLD ALL THESE YEARS. FOR A WRITER, THIS WAS THE GREATEST OF ALL PRICELESS TREASURES.

ONCE I CALMED DOWN AND READ FURTHER, I BEGAN
TO REALIZE THERE WERE TWO UNFATHOMABLY
IMPORTANT THINGS ABOUT THE GHOST BOOK.

THE FIRST:

EDGAR ALLAN POE WAS A MEMBER OF THE
CROSSBONES. TO THINK THAT SOMEHOW, DOWN
THROUGH THE YEARS, I, TOO, WOULD END UP A
CROSSBONES MEMBER — WELL, IT'S JUST UNTHINKABLE.
READING HIS WORDS AS THEY RAN DOWN THE
FIRST TWO PAGES, I FELT TERRIBLY SORRY FOR HIM.
THE CROSSBONES DIDN'T LET POE IN BECAUSE
THEY LIKED HIM. THEY LET HIM IN BECAUSE THEY
FEARED HIM.

Words are my weapon. They want to take them from me. I won't let them!

HE GOES ON TO DESCRIBE A COURTING PERIOD,
WHERE A SECRET SOCIETY INVITED HIM TO SECRET
MEETINGS TO TALK ABOUT SECRET THINGS. BUT HE

KNEW, AFTER A TIME, HOW THEY REALLY FELT. THEY HATED HIM. THEY WANTED TO CRUSH HIM. THEY WANTED TO BURN HIS BOOKS AND SHUT HIM UP. HE WAS BAD FOR AMERICA, BAD FOR THE CHURCH, BAD, BAD, BAD!

They don't know what bad is, these fools! They don't know what it means to suffer.

DECEIVED AND AFRAID, ONLY A FEW MONTHS SHY OF HIS OWN DEATH, POE BEGAN THE GHOST BOOK. HE LEFT NOTES AND SENT LETTERS, TOYING WITH THE CROSSBONES.

There is a book, a book without words. This book, it tells your secrets. Your crimes!

AND SO IT WAS THAT EDGAR ALLAN POE MADE THE CROSSBONES THINK HE'D BETRAYED THEIR

SECRETS, THOUGH WHAT SECRETS HE ACTUALLY KNEW ARE HARD TO SAY. MEMBERS OF THE CROSSBONES ARE PARANOID BY NATURE, AND HE SUCCEEDED (OR SO HE SAYS) IN DRIVING THEM HALF MAD WITH FEAR.

FROM BEYOND THE GRAVE THE BOOK WAS FOUND, BUT POE WAS NOTHING IF NOT GOOD AT BEATING THE CROSSBONES AT THEIR OWN GAME. TO ONE HE GAVE THE WHITE VIAL, TO ANOTHER THE BLACK, AND A THIRD THE GHOST BOOK. HE WHISPERED TO THEM EACH — THE OTHERS CAN'T BE TRUSTED — AND SOON AFTER THAT, EDGAR ALLAN POE WAS DEAD.

THE CROSSBONES, EVER WARY OF THE TRUTH IN THE BOOK, RIPPED THEMSELVES TO SHREDS IN ITS PURSUIT. IF ONLY THEY'D KNOWN THE KEYS WERE ALL HIDDEN WITHIN THEIR OWN RANKS.

LIFE LESSON: DON'T MESS WITH MASTERS OF WORDS. THEY'LL ALWAYS GET YOU IN THE END.

THE SECOND SECRET OF THE GHOST BOOK, A SECRET A THOUSAND TIMES MORE IMPORTANT THAN THE FIRST, IS ONE I CAN SCARCELY BRING MYSELF TO REPORT.

HERE IT IS — SOMETHING REMARKABLE, SOMETHING GRAND.

226

THE PLOY AGAINST THE CROSSBONES LASTED
ONLY TWO PAGES. THE OTHER FORTY PAGES WERE
SOMETHING ELSE.

IT BEGAN ON THE TOP OF THE THIRD PAGE.

*I have a dreadful fear. Of my own death? No, not <u>that</u>
death. It comes for me either way. Fear will credit me
nothing. I fear the death of my words. I fear they'll find
them, burn them, hurl them into the abyss!*

Here I keep them safe. Here they can't be found.

*Drink, world, drink! These secret words I write
for you.*

AND AFTER THAT? WORDS. MANY OF THEM. I SAT
IN MY ROOM AND PAINTED THEM INTO EXISTENCE. IT
WASN'T ONE LONG STORY — NO, IT WAS SOMETHING FAR
GREATER THAN THAT. PAGE AFTER PAGE OF IDEAS,
STORIES HE WANTED TO TELL BUT DIDN'T HAVE THE TIME
FOR. EVERY PAGE IN THE GHOST BOOK WAS THE
SKELETON OF A NEW STORY. AND THE MOST AMAZING
THING OF ALL — A HUNDRED YEARS LATER, I WAS

ENTRANCED BY EVERY IDEA. EACH OF THEM WHOLLY ORIGINAL, EACH OF THEM GHASTLY, GOTHIC, MYSTERIOUS, OR FANTASTIC. STRANGE CREATURES AND CHARACTERS IN PLACES STRANGER STILL, THE MASTER IN HIS LABORATORY, BUILDING A MONSTER BEFORE MY EYES.

I've decided to keep the ghost book. I know what you're thinking: That's a crime. You can't keep it all to yourself. It belongs to everyone, not just you.

I suppose you're right. But I'm still keeping it.

I've been giving a lot of things back to the world lately. I'm just not ready to let this one go. I feel like Gollum in <u>The Lord of the Rings</u>. The ghost book is my precious. I wonder if it will make me live a thousand years and move into a cave and eat raw fish for dinner? Somehow I doubt it.

Hear me out before you judge me.

Edgar Allan Poe didn't have a rich family to lean on or a job to fill his bank account. He believed his writing would be enough.

Poe failed in the end, and part of that failure was his own. No one is saying he didn't dig at least half his own grave. But the world dug the rest, and the Crossbones used a big shovel. One writer to another, I feel like a secret torch has been passed from a master to an apprentice. I feel

LIKE THESE IDEAS WERE HANDED DOWN TO ME, LIKE HE
REACHED HIS HAND INTO THE WORLD FROM THE GREAT
UNKNOWN AND MADE THIS HAPPEN. HE PUT THE GHOST
BOOK AND THE WAY INSIDE IN MY HANDS. I'LL ALWAYS
BELIEVE THAT, NO MATTER WHAT ANYONE SAYS.

I'M GOING TO FINISH WHAT HE STARTED.

SARAH WILL PROBABLY LAUGH AT THIS, AND THAT'S
OKAY. BUT I WANT TO HANG ON TO THESE WORDS FOR
JUST A LITTLE WHILE AND TRY TO TURN THEM INTO
WHAT I THINK HE WOULD HAVE WANTED. I'M NOT GOING
TO USE HIS WORDS, I'M GOING TO USE MINE. AND I'VE
DECIDED SOMETHING ELSE.

I'M GOING TO TELL SARAH AND FITZ ABOUT THE
GHOST BOOK.

THE THREE OF US ARE GOING TO DO THIS
TOGETHER. WE'RE GOING TO TURN THE CROSSBONES
ON ITS HEAD. WE'RE GOING TO MAKE IT INTO
SOMETHING NEW. THIS CROSSBONES WILL NOT BE
ABOUT THE BUSINESS OF KILLING IDEAS AND STORIES AND
BOOKS. IN A TWIST OF FATE ONLY POE HIMSELF COULD
HAVE ORCHESTRATED, THE NEW MEMBERS OF THE
CROSSBONES ARE GOING TO GIVE THE WORLD MORE
OF HIS STORIES, NOT LESS.

I CAN'T HELP WONDERING IF A DAY WILL COME WHEN FITZ IS FORCED TO TAKE UP THE GREAT AX AND PROTECT THE CROSSBONES FROM SOMETHING I CAN'T YET SEE. OR IF SARAH WILL LEAVE SECRET VIDEOS AND PUZZLES FOR TWO CURIOUS TEENAGERS TO FIND. I WONDER IF WE'LL BE AT ODDS WITH ONE ANOTHER SOMEWHERE DOWN THE LINE, IF WE'LL FIGHT FOR POWER. I HOPE THAT WILL NEVER HAPPEN.

IN OUR OWN WAY — A WAY ONLY WE CAN UNDERSTAND — I HOPE WE'LL BE TOGETHER ALWAYS.

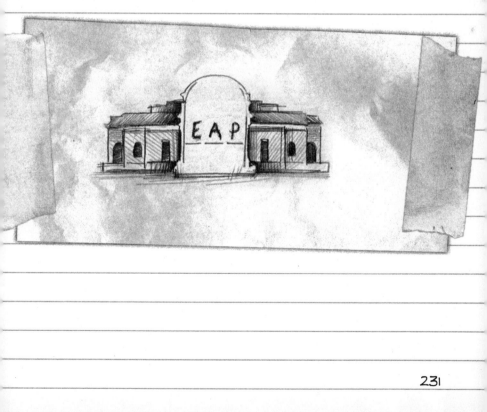

WWW.SARAHFINCHER.COM
PASSWORD:
RESTINPEACE